Ned, the city boy, learned how to ride – and why honesty is best . . .

Jenny discovered the meaning of fear . . .

Joskins the medicine man, got what he deserved . . .

Jonah the donkey was poisoned – and made a lifelong friend . . .

Dolly Waygood made a big mistake when she sneered at the doctor's horse . . .

Kevin rescued a damsel in distress . . .

. . . and through it all the reassuring figure of Black Beauty looked on – helping out where he could, defending the family who looked after him, and joining in the happy endings.

THE AUTHOR

Richard Carpenter trained at the Old Vic Theatre School and worked as an actor for 15 years before taking up writing.

After some short stories for radio he wrote Catweazle, which won the Writers Guild Award in 1971 for the best children's television drama script.

The following year he won the same award, jointly with David Butler, for The Adventures of Black Beauty.

He works as a presenter and scriptwriter for BBC Schools programmes, and his Catweazle books have been translated into five languages.

He is married to the actress Annabelle Lee. They live in London with their two children, Harriet (9) and Tom (12).

The Best of Black Beauty

Richard Carpenter

EVEREST BOOKS LIMITED
4 Valentine Place London SE1

Published in Great Britain by Everest Books Ltd, 1975

ISBN 0903925 788

Based upon the television series 'The Adventures of Black Beauty'

Made and printed in Great Britain by
Hazell Watson & Viney Ltd, Aylesbury, Bucks

CONTENTS

ACKNOWLEDGEMENT

I would like to thank Sidney Cole, Paul Knight, Anthony Gruner, and Max Wilk, who helped me so much with my scripts for the London Weekend International television film series, 'The Adventures of Black Beauty'.

The inspiration for the series was of course, Anna Sewell's classic, and I urge any child – who has not already done so – to read the original 'Black Beauty'.

About a hundred years ago, on the edge of the quiet village of Five Oaks, stood York Cottage, home of Doctor James Gordon and his family.

The doctor was a widower, and he and his children were looked after by Miss Amy Winthrop, who was their housekeeper. Amy had been with them so long she was one of the family.

But someone else was also very much part of the Gordon household. Someone who was loved by everyone. The doctor's noble horse, Black Beauty.

This book tells some of the adventures of Black Beauty in that Victorian countryside of long ago.

CHAPTER ONE

THE OUTCAST

It was a cold clear morning in early spring and Black Beauty was munching contentedly at some sweet hay in the musty warmth of his stable when Ned Lewis ran in and slammed the door. The boy was pale and trembling and looked around fearfully. For somewhere to hide. Beauty heard footsteps running across the yard; then the stable door was thrown open again and Doctor Gordon strode in with Kevin and Jenny. They looked accusingly at the frightened boy. 'Empty your pockets, Ned!' said James quietly.

Ned backed away as Amy joined the little group by the door.

'He's got it father – I know he has,' said Kevin.

Only Black Beauty could see Ned was holding a clasp knife behind his back; he lowered his head and nuzzled at the boy's hand. Ned – who had forgotten the horse was standing behind him – started guiltily and dropped the knife.

For a moment everyone stared at it then Kevin picked it up and put it in his pocket without a word. It was Ned who finally broke the silence. 'I only wanted to borrow it,' he said lamely.

'You've a knife of your own,' retorted Kevin with disgust. 'You were going to sell it!'

Amy looked sadly at her nephew. 'Is that true, Ned?' she asked.

'What about my magnifying glass?' accused Kevin. 'And the other things?'

'You said you wouldn't tell—'

'You said you wouldn't steal again!'

Doctor Gordon waited patiently for Ned's explanation: the boy's behaviour was becoming a serious problem.

'Are yer goin' ter beat me?' Ned asked, still refusing to admit his guilt.

'No,' said James, much to the boy's astonishment, 'you'd better puzzle out why you steal, Ned. And a sore behind won't help you to do that.'

Ned found this hard to understand, but then he found most things in Five Oaks hard to understand. He wasn't used to the country. The quiet nights frightened him; so did the cows and sheep and the other animals, especially Black Beauty.

He was a city boy. His mother had died leaving him destitute; and so he had joined the small army of beggars and thieves who lived by their wits in the narrow streets and alleys near the London docks. This bad company had undone all the notions of honesty and straight dealing he'd been taught, so when at last he was found by his Aunt Amy, and brought to York Cottage, his ideas of right and wrong were very confused.

'I ain't going to be punished?' Ned was bewildered.

'Oh yes, Ned – you'll be punished,' said James.

Ned tilted his chin defiantly: 'When?'

'Whenever anyone finds it hard to trust you,' replied James quietly.

For a moment Ned looked at them all: he could feel

himself reddening with guilt. Suddenly he could face them no longer.

Out he ran; out of the dark stable with its strange country smells, and across the yard – scattering the chickens before him. Like a cat he leapt to the top of the yard wall then dropped to the ground and raced to the freedom of the woods and fields beyond.

'Let him go,' said James. 'He'll be back. He needs time to think things out.'

But Ned was not thinking at all. He ran heedlessly, desperation boiling within him, urging him on until he could run no further. Then he looked down the hillside to where York Cottage nestled at the edge of the village.

'Keep yer charity!' he shouted. 'I don't want it! I wish there was a bloomin' great earthquake and you was all swallered up! All of yer!'

His rage ebbed away leaving him empty, almost numb. Then he recovered his breath and spoke quietly. 'I wish there was nobody alive but me. Nobody.'

The distant cottage was to him a symbol of all that was safe, all that was warm and friendly. It was a family place, and he felt he could have no part of it. He was an outcast. The comfortable feather-beds of York Cottage were not for him. His bed was the cold stone step of a locked doorway.

And so, feeling very sorry for himself, and quite sure the whole world was united against him, Ned walked slowly into the woods. He picked up a stick and swished moodily at the undergrowth. On he went, little caring where, aimlessly following the twisting paths which led him deeper into the woods, while he brooded on his humiliation in the stables. Presently he began to daydream, as he walked along. He would run away to sea and only return after many adventures, with money to burn and servants to command. He was boarding a pirate ship in the China Seas, when he saw something in the wood ahead which ended his daydream abruptly.

Tied to a tree by the side of the path, was a very small white pony, its bright red saddle and bridle decorated with silver stars. On its head it wore a plume of red feathers, and, as Ned approached, he could see tiny bells hanging from its trappings.

He had never seen anything like it before, and for a moment thought he was dreaming. He tiptoed towards it as if afraid it might vanish into thin air. As he reached it, a tall, cadaverous-looking man rose from the undergrowth.

'Leave 'im be! Leave 'im be – you young devil!'

Ned backed away in alarm. The man looked dangerous, and carried a heavy stick.

'What's yer game – eh?'

'Nothing mister. I ain't seen such a little 'orse before – that's all.'

'Oh, 'aven't yer?' sneered the man as he began to untie the pony, eyeing Ned with considerable suspicion.

But Ned's curiosity overcame his fear. 'What's 'is name?' he asked.

'Jonah,' snapped the man. 'And a right Jonah he's turned out to be!'

'Why's he got up so fancy? What's all them bells for?' Ned had a sudden idea. 'Hey – you ain't stealed 'im from a circus – 'ave yer?'

The man raised his stick menacingly. 'You clear off! Go on! Clear off!' He grabbed little Jonah's bridle and gave it a savage tug. 'Come on, you good-for-nothing brute!'

But Jonah would not move. The man went on tugging cruelly until Ned could bear it no longer.

'Er – steady on!' he exclaimed.

The man stopped pulling at Jonah's bridle. 'What did you say!' he said.

'You're 'urting 'im!'

The man flushed, angrily, and raised his stick high into the air. 'I told you to clear off!' he roared, and began raining blows on Ned's unprotected shoulders.

Ned took to his heels while the man shouted curses after him. Jonah, finding himself no longer the centre of his owner's cruel attentions, trotted away in the opposite direction, the bells jingling on his harness as he disappeared among the trees.

But Ned saw none of this. He fled through the undergrowth, the thorns and brambles tearing at his clothes.

He stopped running, realised that his attacker was not following and flopped down on a tree stump to review the situation. He was very puzzled.

'Do something wrong – and you don't get beaten,' he said shaking his head. 'Do something right – and you do!'

Back at York Cottage, the family were beginning to get worried about him. Kevin offered to go and look for him. 'He won't have got far,' he said. 'Let me take Beauty.'

'I think I'd better try, Kevin,' said Doctor Gordon.

'But I know the woods. I know all the places he might hide.'

'Suppose he won't come back with you?'

'He'll come if he's hungry enough,' grinned Kevin. 'Please let me try.'

His son's concern for the wayward Ned touched Doctor Gordon deeply, and he agreed finally to let him go.

Kevin mounted Black Beauty and cantered out of the yard, and James turned to Amy. 'I only hope that lad's kept away from the marshes,' he said.

'That lad' was not worrying about the marshes. He was lost and beginning to feel rather hungry. He looked around for some berries to eat but he couldn't find any. As it was Spring this was hardly surprising. Disappointed he trudged on, getting more and more tired, and feeling very empty. There was a ringing in his ears and he was sure he was about to faint. The ringing grew louder. Then he realised that it wasn't in his head at all. It was coming from the bushes, and after a moment, Jonah trotted into view.

Ned wanted nothing to do with him. 'Go away!' he said. 'Shoo! shoo!'

The little pony put his head on one side and looked questioningly at him. The red plumes danced in the wind and the little bells tinkled merrily. He nuzzled at Ned's hand.

'I ain't got nothin' for yer,' said Ned, reminded of his own hunger. 'Ain't got nothin' for meself come ter that. Go on – shoo! Shoo!' But Jonah wouldn't shoo; the boy had helped him escape from his cruel master, and he wanted to stay with him. And when Ned walked on, he trotted after him.

Ned turned. 'Don't you understand English! Leave me alone! Get away from me! I don't want yer – see? I don't want no one.'

But Jonah didn't, or wouldn't, understand. Whenever Ned began to run, Jonah trotted after him and Ned just couldn't shake him off. However hard he ran, the jingling of the little bells was always behind him. Finally he gave up trying to get away and collapsed wearily. He looked helplessly at Jonah. 'Don't you ever give up?' he groaned. 'Don't you know you ain't wanted? eh?'

But Jonah merely whinnied happily. He had no idea Ned was rejecting him.

'If you bring that crazy master of yours down on me again, I'll . . . I'll . . .' Ned looked at the trailing bridle. Then he got up and led Jonah to the nearest tree. 'I'm going to London, mate,' he said, as he tethered him, 'and you ain't comin'.'

Jonah looked sadly after Ned as he hurried away; then he began to chew determinedly at the bridle.

Some time later a tired and dispirited Ned could hardly believe it when he heard the tinkling of bells and Jonah again caught up with him. Despite his weariness he broke into a run in an effort to escape from his four-footed pursuer; and, not looking where he was going, stumbled straight into a treacherous patch of quagmire.

Thrashing about in an effort to free himself he shouted angrily at Jonah, who had very sensibly stopped on firm ground. 'You jinglin' juggins! Look what you made me do!'

Jonah calmly began to eat the grass.

'Fine time to 'ave yer dinner!' yelled Ned, struggling to free himself. Soon, however, he was up to his knees and his anger with Jonah gave way to a very real fear. He fought wildly to get out. But the more he fought, the deeper he sank. 'Help!' he cried. 'Help!'

Then, quite suddenly, Jonah stopped eating grass and, turning away, trotted off the way he'd come, leaving Ned still in desperate trouble.

Meanwhile, Kevin, riding Black Beauty, had entered the wood to begin his search. But neither of them had expected to find a gaily harnessed Shetland pony. Jonah trotted across a clearing towards them and did everything he could to make them follow him, even going up on his hind legs and executing a graceful pirouette – a trick he'd learnt in the circus. At last Kevin understood. 'He wants us to follow him,' he whispered as Jonah started to lead them back to Ned.

When they heard Ned's frantic cries for help, Black Beauty quickened his pace.

'Stop struggling, you idiot!' said Kevin as he dismounted and squatted down by the patch of quagmire.

'But I'll go under!' wailed Ned.

'You will if you don't stop thrashing about!'

'You'll never pull me out.'

'No,' said Kevin, 'but Beauty will.'

Jonah watched carefully as Kevin led Black Beauty to the edge of the firm ground and lengthened one of his stirrup leathers. 'Grab hold!' he commanded.

Ned stretched his arm towards the stirrup and after a great effort he managed to grasp it. Then Beauty moved slowly away and he was dragged to safety.

He was covered with evil smelling mud and it was some time before he was able to get shakily to his feet. 'All right,' said Kevin. 'Now let's go home.'

'What 'ome? I ain't got one,' said Ned defiantly. He tried to run but Kevin brought him crashing to the ground. They rolled over and over, each trying to get the upper hand, and very soon Kevin was as muddy as Ned. They fought in silence, watched impassively by Black Beauty and Jonah, until at last, Kevin managed to sit on Ned's chest, pinning him to the ground. They were both panting after their battle. Ned glared up at Kevin. 'I ain't coming back,' he gasped. 'You can't make me—'

'Where did you get that pony?'

'It ain't nothing to do with me.'

'You stole it – didn't you?'

'No I never,' said Ned indignantly. 'It followed me. It won't go away!'

'Followed you!' cried Kevin incredulously. 'Do you really expect me to believe that?'

Ned squirmed beneath him. 'Let me get up,' he pleaded. 'I promise you I won't try to run for it.'

Kevin let him up, though he went on watching him as warily as any wrestler. He listened disbelievingly to the story of Jonah. 'Why would I steal a thing like that?' Ned concluded, gesturing with a muddy hand towards the little pony standing in the protective shadow of Black Beauty.

'To sell it of course,' Kevin answered, scornfully. 'So you could get to London.'

Doctor Gordon had been right, thought Ned bitterly; this *was* his punishment. No one would ever trust him again. He turned away in despair. But before he had gone more than a few yards, there was a jingling of bells and Jonah was by his side again. Kevin stared in amazement. Ned had been telling the truth after all; the pony *had* followed him.

'Wait, Ned!' he called. 'I believe you. Jonah's just proved it.'

Ned smiled at the little pony. Then he stroked his mane. 'Thanks, Jonah,' he said softly.

'I'm sorry,' said Kevin and held out his hand.

'I'm sorry too,' said Ned. 'I'm sorry I stole your things.'

Very solemnly, the two of them shook hands.

'What are we going to do about 'im?' said Ned.

'Find his owner,' said Kevin, who was a practical boy.

'But what if we can't!' said Ned – who didn't really want to.

'Father would know what to do,' said Kevin quietly, looking keenly at Ned, who understood the meaning behind these words. Kevin was asking him to abandon his idea of running away. 'I'd have been half way to London by now, if it hadn't been for you,' he muttered ruefully to Jonah. But Kevin was right – there was nowhere else he could go. So with Black Beauty to guide them, they began to make their way back home.

They put Black Beauty and Jonah in the stable. The two boys were covered in mud, and hoped nobody would see them until they had managed to clean themselves up. They were sneaking somewhat guiltily from the stable when a sudden shout stopped them. Coming across the yard was Doctor Gordon and by his side was the tall, cruel-looking man Ned had encountered in the wood. The man raised his stick and pointed it at Ned. 'That's him!' he shouted angrily. 'That's the young thief that stole my pony!'

CHAPTER TWO

THE QUARRY

In vain Ned tried to account for Jonah's presence in the stable. Kevin tried too, but Doctor Gordon was in no mood to listen to either of them; and the pony's owner, Mr. Randall, kept on muttering and interrupting and making it quite impossible for either boy to be heard. In the end Doctor Gordon lost his temper and locked Ned in his bedroom even though Kevin continued to protest his innocence.

Jonah was handed over to Mr. Randall who told the Gordons how his brother, who had worked in a circus, had left him the pony in his will. 'I'd have sooner 'ad the money he owed me,' he muttered.

Then he said he wanted Ned put in jail for stealing Jonah. 'He's a horse thief, ain't he?' he whined.

But Doctor Gordon quickly dismissed this vindictive idea. 'He's in my charge, Mr. Randall,' he said firmly. 'And I will deal with him.'

Randall was cowed by Doctor Gordon's firm manner, so he began pulling the unwilling Jonah away from the cottage. 'Come on you,' he muttered savagely. 'It's a fair walk to Eddington Hall.'

'Why are you taking him there?' asked Kevin.

'Why do you think?' retorted Randall with a sneer – 'to sell him of course.'

Kevin watched sadly as the man disappeared down the

road tugging the reluctant little pony. Jonah neighed a pathetic goobye to Black Beauty who stamped angrily seeing Randall's harsh treatment of his new friend.

Kevin tried yet again to plead Ned's innocence but his father would not listen. Even Amy, who was always so patient and understanding, would not listen, and so finally, Kevin found himself alone with Black Beauty. He smiled at the powerful horse. Beauty knew the truth of the matter. 'I wish you could tell them,' whispered Kevin. 'They might listen to you.'

Beauty moved restlessly and it seemed to Kevin that he was shaking his head in disagreement. Then suddenly Kevin knew what they had to do. They had to prove Ned's innocence. But first he had to be released from his unfair imprisonment.

Very carefully, Kevin placed a ladder against the wall of the cottage under Ned's open window. He threw up a couple of pebbles and Ned looked out. 'Come on down!' hissed Kevin.

'No! I'm in enough trouble.'

'It's my fault.'

'No it ain't,' said Ned. 'It's mine.'

Kevin sighed with exasperation. 'We haven't got time to argue,' he said. 'Come on down!'

Ned hesitated for a moment, wondering why Kevin was engineering his escape. After all, he wasn't really one of the family and yet here was Kevin defying his own father to help him. It was all very puzzling. 'What's the game?' said Ned as he climbed down the ladder.

'I'll join you later,' said Kevin.

'Yes but—'

'Go on!' ordered Kevin, and watched him race for the

shelter of the trees. Some minutes later, mounted on Black Beauty, he arrived at Ned's hiding place.

'We're going to get Randall to tell father the truth,' said Kevin, jumping off Beauty and giving Ned some bread and cheese he'd filched from the kitchen.

'You're barmy,' Ned mumbled as he ate. 'How do you think you're going to do that?'

'I don't know,' admitted Kevin, 'but perhaps if he could see how Jonah follows you, even when you tell him not to, he might believe you.'

'It's a waste of time,' sighed Ned, 'he's made up his mind. Everybody has. I reckon that once you've been branded a thief, there ain't nothin' that'll change it.'

Kevin was very upset by such cynicism and lack of hope. For the first time he realised how Ned's unhappy background had affected him. Kevin's had been so secure that he had found it hard to understand the rebellious boy from the city who was so full of hate and distrust. Ned was very like Jonah. Ned's harsh life, before he had come to Five Oaks, could be compared with the harsh way Randall had treated the pony since he had taken him from the circus.

'Get up behind me,' ordered Kevin.

'Me get on that thing!' said Ned fearfully. 'No fear. I'll walk, matey!'

Eddington Hall was a Georgian manor house set in a splendidly landscaped park in the middle of a big estate. Here lived Squire Armstrong, the young and rather arrogant owner of all this land and property. He believed in the doubtful Victorian virtues of unquestioning obedience, position, and wealth. He regarded everyone who worked on his estate as a piece of property, and he expected a suitably servile attitude from them. He was constantly annoyed by Doctor Gordon's kindness, and disliked the Gordon children intensely. On several occasions he had stopped Kevin and Jenny riding Black Beauty across his land, even though they had been carefully keeping to the bridle paths.

Squire Armstrong's sister Elizabeth and her daughter Alice were staying with him at Eddington Hall. Little Alice, who was nine, had pestered her uncle to buy her a pony. And finally, worn down by her entreaties, the Squire had begun to ask around the district to see if anyone had a suitably small and docile pony they wished to sell. Randall had seen this as a heaven-sent opportunity to make some money and get rid of his tiresome inheritance. He met Alice and her mother as he was crossing the park. Alice looked at Jonah with joy in her eyes. He was just what she wanted. Her mother, however, was a trifle timid and didn't really want Alice to have a pony at all.

'Jonah's perfect for her, M'am,' said Randall giving Elizabeth what he imagined to be an ingratiating grin.

Elizabeth fluttered nervously. 'You don't think she's too young?' she said.

'Bless you no,' Randall laughed reassuringly. 'Jonah's as gentle as a lamb. Let her have a ride on him and you'll see.'

Elizabeth fiddled with her parasol. 'I really think we should wait for my brother and get his opinion.'

But Randall wasn't going to wait, and lifted the willing Alice into the saddle. Then, giving Jonah a fierce tug, he led the delighted child round her mother. 'Look, Mama! look, I'm riding!' crowed Alice.

But her mother was very unhappy about it. She didn't

like Randall and she didn't trust him either. She also thought that Jonah had rather a nasty look about him; a stubborn look, a look that suggested he might be very unpredictable.

'Let go!' Alice ordered Mr. Randall. 'I want to ride him by myself.' She threw a pleading glance at her mother.

'She can't come to any harm,' Randall said as Jonah began to trot gently across the grass.

Now Alice, who was a rather spoilt and impatient little girl, began banging her heels against Jonah's sides instead of squeezing with her legs as a good rider should. At the same time she pulled on the reins so that the bit hurt his already tender mouth. Poor Jonah didn't know what he was supposed to do! But in the end he decided that he'd had enough of Alice's rough treatment and so he got the bit between his teeth and began to trot as fast as he could. Alice was bounced up and down in the saddle and became very frightened. She called to the pony to stop but Jonah wouldn't obey. He had the bit between his teeth and though Alice hauled hard on the reins, it had no effect on Jonah's headlong flight.

'For heavens sake do something!' screamed Elizabeth. 'She can't ride!'

Randall began chasing after Jonah, shouting at the top of his voice; but the sound of his hateful master only served to make him increase his pace, and by the time Randall reached the park gate, Jonah had vanished.

He stood in the road trembling with fear; if anything happened to Alice, he knew Squire Armstrong would make him suffer for it, and he cursed Jonah from the bottom of his cruel heart. He was still cursing when Kevin appeared on Black Beauty, with Ned walking beside him.

23

Panic-stricken, Randall pointed feverishly down the road. 'Jonah!' he gasped. 'He's run away and Squire Armstrong's niece is riding him!'

For a moment Ned hesitated then he took Kevin's proffered hand, swung himself up behind him, and Black Beauty set off after Jonah.

They found the little pony standing quietly on the path which led along the edge of the stone quarry. But there was no sign of Alice. Kevin and Ned dismounted, quite certain that the little girl had been thrown to the bottom of the quarry.

It was Black Beauty who drew their attention to a faint sobbing. Ned peered over the edge and could see Alice crouched on a narrow ledge a few yards below them. Some bushes growing from the rocks, had stopped her fall but she was in very great danger.

'What are we going to do?' asked Kevin.

'Sssh! not so loud,' said Ned, 'we gotter keep her calm.' Ned approached the edge carefully, lay on his stomach, and peered down at Alice. The little girl looked up at him.

'It's all right,' said Ned softly. 'It's all right. We're getting help. Just try to keep still.'

Alice nodded tearfully; Ned could tell she was very frightened. 'That's it – keep very still, and breathe nice and easy.'

He rejoined Kevin. 'I'm goin' to climb down to 'er,' he said. 'She can't 'old on much longer.'

'You can't do that!' said Kevin. 'What if she panics? She could pull you off with her.'

'Look,' said Ned earnestly. 'I'm lighter than you. That

ledge don't look too safe to me. Besides you can ride and I don't know the way back to Eddington Hall.'

Alice had begun to cry. 'All right, all right,' called Ned. 'Don't cry. I'm comin' down.'

Kevin knew Ned had made up his mind. Together, they wriggled to the edge, where Ned turned and began to lower himself, gripping Kevin's hand. He scrabbled around, finally managing to find a foothold. There was a branch to one side and he grabbed at it. Slowly he let go of Kevin's other hand and then climbed down the remaining feet to the ledge, while Kevin watched anxiously from above.

Ned edged his way to Alice's side. She looked trustingly at him, her face pale and streaked with tears; and very gently Ned took her hand. 'What's yer name, eh?'

'Alice,' said the little girl and started to look down.

'Don't do that!' said Ned quickly. He put his arm round her and called up to Kevin. 'Hurry!' he said.

Kevin wriggled back from the edge and ran up the slope to Black Beauty; and as he rode him away from the quarry, the horse sensed the urgency of their mission and galloped with all his strength.

Jonah watched them go. He was going to stay with Ned, who was doing his best to keep Alice as calm and as still as possible.

'Look – if you – if you keep still, I'll – I'll tell you a story. But you've gotter promise not to move.'

Alice nodded and squeezed his hand, while from above them came a little neigh. Ned smiled ruefully; in a way it was all Jonah's fault.

'Well then,' he began, 'once upon a time there was this boy, see. His name was Ned, and sometimes – only some-

Just as the rest of the ledge broke away.

times mind – he sort of – well – took things. What didn't actcherly belong to him—' He broke off in alarm. Part of the ledge was beginning to crumble away . . .

Kevin met Squire Armstrong and his men on the road to Eddington Hall. 'She's trapped on a ledge,' he gasped. Then he turned Black Beauty and raced back to the quarry with the Squire and his men behind him.

They were only just in time. Great lumps of the ledge were breaking away and sliding to the quarry below.

The Squire's men threw a rope down to Ned. Swiftly he tied it round the terrified Alice and she was hauled to safety. Down came the rope again and Ned was pulled up just as the rest of the ledge broke away and avalanched down to the bottom of the quarry.

Back at Eddington Hall, Squire Armstrong angrily ordered Randall to get out of his sight and take Jonah with him. But he gave each of the boys a golden sovereign for their bravery.

'Is Jonah still for sale?' said Kevin, as Randall hurried away, still tugging the reluctant pony.

'Don't make fun of me, boy,' he snarled.

Kevin took Ned's sovereign from his hand and held out the two of them to Randall. 'Will this buy him?' he asked.

Randall looked at the money; the boy was obviously mad. He couldn't believe his luck. 'Done!' he said grabbing at the sovereigns.

'Here!' said Ned, totally bewildered. 'Half of that was mine!'

'All of it was,' said Kevin putting Jonah's gaily coloured bridle into Ned's hand. 'You've just bought a pony!'

Ned was astonished. What was Kevin thinking of? He didn't want Jonah! He dropped the bridle and ran off

27

down the road as fast as he could. Jonah pricked up his ears and set off after him.

Black Beauty and the others watched them both disappear until all that could be heard was the faint tinkling of little bells.

Ned never stole again; and, as the weeks passed, he realised that he really was 'one of the family' and an outcast no longer. And Jonah had the master he wanted!

CHAPTER THREE

SECRET OF FEAR

Nothing in the world gave Jenny Gordon more joy than to be allowed to ride Black Beauty. He responded instantly to her slightest command, and when he jumped Jenny felt she was flying. She loved the freedom of a long gallop over the fields; and Beauty loved it too. She would often deliver her father's prescriptions because it gave her the chance to ride Black Beauty.

Jenny was returning to York Cottage from just such an errand, when she learnt that a jumping competition was to be held at a nearby village. When she asked Doctor Gordon if she could enter Black Beauty, he smiled his assent. Albert – a local boy who was a friend of Jenny and Kevin, and who practically lived at York Cottage – gave a snort of derision.

'You're horse mad – that's what you are,' he said. 'You want to be careful. My cousin was just the same, poor feller!'

Albert was famous for his rather tall stories; Doctor Gordon winked at Jenny. 'Why – what happened to him?' he enquired innocently.

Albert looked serious. 'He thought he *was* a horse, in the end. And they found him one morning – galloping round a field with a saddle on his back.'

'And were they able to help him?' asked Doctor Gordon – equally serious.

Albert's eyes widened. 'Help him? Why, he came fourth in the Derby!'

They were still laughing when a stranger rode up to them. He was young and very pale, and there was an indefinable air of menace about him; as if he possessed a mysterious and dangerous knowledge. His eyes, which were very dark, had an intense and disturbing quality. He explained that he was the son of William Duncan, who had been a friend of Doctor Gordon's at Edinburgh University.

'I've come to ask a favour, Doctor Gordon,' said young Mr. Duncan.

'Ask away,' replied James politely.

But young Duncan made it clear that he didn't want to say anything in front of Jenny and Albert, so James took him into the cottage. Duncan explained that though he was not fully qualified, he had the opportunity to become the personal physician to a rich old lady who lived nearby. All he needed was a letter of recommendation.

'But I cannot recommend someone I don't know,' said Doctor Gordon. 'And the fact that you're not fully qualified makes it out of the question.'

'I've been studying abroad,' retorted Duncan angrily. 'They're years ahead of this country. Why, they've methods of treating nervous disorders, for instance, that an ordinary G.P. like you couldn't begin to understand.'

James stood up. 'Then I don't see why such a clever young man wants to waste his time on old Lady Wainwright.'

Duncan was about to reply but James cut in. 'Oh, I'm sure she'll pay you very well, and you'll have plenty of leisure, because – as everyone knows – there's nothing really wrong with her.'

'Just what are you suggesting?' said Duncan coldly.

'I'm suggesting that you complete your proper training and become a real doctor like your father, instead of a rich old lady's pet.'

For a moment Duncan glared at Doctor Gordon as if he was going to strike him. Then, without a word, he left the room, slamming the door behind him.

Albert was sitting on the paddock fence, watching Jenny taking Black Beauty over some improvised jumps, when Duncan marched angrily up and untethered his horse. 'Horse mad, she is,' repeated Albert. Duncan, about to ride off, paused and looked at Jenny on Black Beauty. He would teach Doctor Gordon a lesson he would never forget. Then with his face pale and set with anger he rode away from York Cottage.

Albert watched him go as Jenny cantered over to the rail. 'Reckon your father upset him,' said Albert. 'He's real angry about something. He's a nasty piece of work if you ask me.'

A few days later, Jenny and Albert were playing hide and seek in the woods when Jenny suddenly came face to face with young Mr. Duncan. He smiled at her and raised his hat politely. 'Ah, Miss Gordon! Might I have a word with you?' he said softly.

Albert, who was bored because Jenny had not found him, came back to where he'd left her, in time to see Duncan walking away. Jenny was standing motionless. 'I've been hiding for hours,' said Albert indignantly. 'You didn't even try to find me! What did he want, anyway?'

'Who?'

31

'Who?' repeated Albert. 'Why, Duncan, of course.'

Jenny looked rather dazed. 'Oh . . . yes . . . nothing . . .'

'Nothing?' said Albert, puzzled by Jenny's strange manner.

'He . . . talked about Black Beauty . . . that's all . . .'

Later that same day Jenny took a bucket of water to Black Beauty in his stable. As he turned to greet her, she became afraid. She backed away, dropping the bucket on to the straw. Her throat was dry with terror; she was so frightened she found it hard to breathe. Finally, she began to scream and ran out into the yard. She stumbled towards the kitchen door, holding her face in her hands – sobbing desperately. Doctor Gordon and Amy – who had heard the scream – ran up to her. Jenny buried her face against her father, crying hysterically.

'What's happened?' asked the doctor urgently. 'Jenny – what's happened?'

Jenny continued to sob in her father's arms while Amy ran to the stable to see if anything had happened to Black Beauty. Reassured, she returned to find Jenny still struggling to speak.

'I'm – I'm – so – frightened!' she finally choked out. James crouched down and took her hands. He looked up at her. 'All right. All right,' he said, doing his best to calm her, 'Tell me. Tell me what it is.'

'It's – it's – him!'

'Who, child?' whispered Amy gently, putting a protective arm around the trembling girl's shoulders.

Jenny spun round to face the stable, and pointed towards it, her arm trembling. 'Him!' she screamed, and once again burst into tears, covering her face in her hands.

Doctor Gordon and Amy looked at one another in

dismay. Why should Jenny be frightened of Black Beauty? It didn't make sense. But Doctor Gordon knew that this was no time to question her, and so he led the weeping girl indoors and she was put to bed.

The next morning there was a knock at her door. Albert peered in and gave Jenny a very wary look.

'It's all right,' said Jenny sadly. 'I'm not dangerous.'

Albert pulled up a chair and looked at her with what he thought was his best professional manner. 'It's the high strikes. That's what you've got.'

'Hysterics,' Jenny corrected. 'And I haven't, anyway.'

'My Granny had 'em,' went on Albert, ignoring Jenny's interruption. 'Granddad used to chuck water over 'er.'

'Did it cure her?'

'No. Just gave her a bad cold,' replied Albert gravely.

There was a neigh from Black Beauty who moved restlessly in the field below, and Jenny cowered away from the sound. 'He's just as worried about you as the rest of us,' said Albert, surprised and shaken by her reaction. He closed the window and then watched as Doctor Gordon led Black Beauty away. It was as if the horse knew that something was wrong and was trying to tell Jenny he would never harm her.

'You've been bewitched if you ask me,' said Albert darkly.

'I suppose you think an evil magician put a spell on me,' sighed Jenny, who was used to Albert's flights of fancy.

Then Albert remembered Mr. Duncan. He rose and began to pace up and down, his doctor role replaced by that of the great detective.

'That man Duncan,' he said, thinking out loud, 'there's something odd about him, if you ask me. What did he say to you about Beauty? You know, in the woods – when we were playing hide and seek.'

'He wasn't in the woods.'

'Yes he was! – You were talking to him! I saw you!'

Jenny stared at Albert. It was obvious to him that Jenny had no recollection of the meeting, and yet he had seen her with Duncan. Albert tried hard to remember something he had read in one of his favourite 'Penny Dreadfuls'. It nagged at his mind but he couldn't recall it.

'I'm going to find Duncan,' said the great detective.

The Two Foxes stood facing the village green, shaded by one of the five great oak trees which gave the village its name. It was a very popular inn, and when Albert rode up on Black Beauty, the forecourt was crowded with villagers, and workers from outlying farms. Albert had learnt from the village blacksmith – a very reliable source of information – that Duncan was staying at the Two Foxes.

Leaving Black Beauty to quench his thirst at the water trough, Albert tried to slip through the door. But he was stopped by the landlord. 'Where d'you think you're going?' he said.

'To see Mr. Duncan,' replied Albert glibly. 'I've got an appointment.'

'Have you indeed?' said the landlord, blocking his way. 'Well, Doctor Duncan's out. Ridden over to see Lady Wainwright.'

Albert waited until his back was turned and darted into the inn.

No one saw him as he crept cautiously up the wooden stairs. After peeping through a few keyholes, he decided on what seemed to him the most likely room. The table was littered with papers and there were several large books. One in particular drew his attention. It was a book about hypotism. There was a bookmark in it and Albert opened it carefully. 'In certain highly responsive subjects – usually young women or girls – it is possible to induce fear of familiar objects,' he read aloud.

'A horse for instance—' said Duncan's voice behind him.

Albert spun round as Duncan pushed the bedroom door shut, folded his arms and smiled evilly at him.

CHAPTER FOUR

THE HYPNOTIST

'Yes,' said Duncan, 'I have studied hypnotism. Doctor Gordon's daughter will never ride again because every time she sees or hears a horse, she'll become terrified.'

'But why hypnotise Jenny?' gasped Albert.

'To teach her father a lesson,' breathed Duncan.

'You can't let her stay like that!'

'Who's going to stop me?'

'I will. I'll tell.'

Duncan began to move towards Albert menacingly. 'I don't think you will,' he said softly. He held out his hand and showed Albert a large ring he was wearing. 'Look at this ring, boy,' he whispered. 'Isn't it beautiful? See how it flashes and sparkles . . .'

Albert looked at the ring. The stone flashed brilliantly, making his eyes water. His eyelids began to droop and he suddenly felt very tired. Duncan's voice seemed to be coming from a long way off. 'Flashes . . . and sparkles . . . flashes . . . and sparkles . . .'

Duncan touched Albert's shoulder and the boy sat obediently.

But the next second Albert shot to his feet – very wide awake and aware of danger. He'd nearly succeeded.

'You're tryin' to hypnotise me – ain't you? So I forget all about it. So I forget everything you've told me!'

36

'Look at the ring . . .' breathed Duncan, flashing it again and again in Albert's eyes.

'Shan't!' said Albert.

'Look at the ring!'

'You look at it!'

'You're feeling drowsy . . . very drowsy . . .'

'No I ain't,' said Albert stubbornly, 'I'm very wide awake!'

Duncan redoubled his efforts. The boy was by no means an easy subject. 'You want to sleep . . . to sleep . . .' Albert took refuge in poety. ' "The boy stood on the burnin' deck. Whence all but he had fled," ' he recited loudly and firmly.

Duncan was very disconcerted by Albert's lightning burst of verse but he recovered swiftly. 'Sleep . . .' he intoned, 'sleep . . . sleep . . .'

' "Augustus was a chubby lad. Fat ruddy cheeks Augustus had," ' recited Albert with cheerful determination, switching to Strüwelpeter.

Duncan began to lose his temper. 'You will do everything I say,' he said trying hard to gain mastery over Albert's will.

Albert decided to adopt a different tack. His eyes flickered shut as he pretended to be hypnotised. 'Everything you say,' he repeated in a monotone.

'You will sleep . . .' murmured Duncan not quite sure that Albert was really going under.

'Sleep . . .' repeated Albert dutifully, 'Sit down,' ordered Duncan, 'sit down, my boy . . .'

Albert did as he was told and began to breathe heavily. Duncan relaxed and straightening up, stood back and wiped his brow. It had been quite a battle. There was a decanter of wine standing on the table and he poured himself a glass. Albert opened one eye and, seeing Duncan occupied, seized his opportunity and made for the door.

He took the stairs three at a time with Duncan right behind him. At the door he cannoned into the landlord, returning with a tray of empty glasses. There was a crash of glass and a roar of anger from the landlord, but Albert kept going. He barged his way past the drinking villagers, leapt on to Black Beauty and galloped across the village green, while Duncan ran for his horse. The trees flashed past and Black Beauty's hooves drummed on the dusty road. The spendid horse galloped like the wind. Albert was sure that, at such a speed, Duncan had little chance of catching him. He was tearing through the woods when he glanced back to see if Duncan was in sight. Riding through woodlands at such a breakneck pace is very dangerous. And so it proved for Albert. As he turned, he crashed into a low branch which swept him from the saddle and sent him spinning to the ground unconscious.

Beauty halted quickly and trotted back to where his young rider lay. Bending his head he snuffled at the boy's body. But Albert did not move. Beauty became agitated and stamped restlessly. He threw back his head and whinnied loudly, his danger signal echoing through the trees. Albert was hurt and Beauty's instinct told him to seek help at York Cottage. His many rides with the children had taught him every path through the woods, every track and every field in the surrounding countryside. He sniffed the air, sensing the way home, and then galloped off leaving Albert pale and motionless.

Ironically, Duncan had abandoned the chase and returned to the Two Foxes. He consoled himself with the

At the door he cannoned into the landlord.

thought that no one was likely to believe Albert's wild tale of hypnotism.

Doctor Gordon and Amy had gone visiting, and so Jenny was alone when Black Beauty galloped up to the cottage. He whickered a friendly greeting but once again Jenny found herself trembling with fear and began backing away in terror. She ran inside the cottage and upstairs to her room, where she flung herself down on the bed and wept bitterly.

Black Beauty stood sadly looking up at her window. Why did she fear him so? He wanted her help. He wanted to take her to Albert. He neighed loudly trying hard to make her understand but this only made Jenny more frightened, and she covered her ears to shut out the sound.

Black Beauty cantered round the cottage, neighing wildly, desperately trying to get Jenny to come to him. He needed her friendship, and was worried by her rejection. He called to her again and again but she would not come.

When he saw Doctor Gordon and Amy, coming across the fields, he galloped up to them. They had heard his frantic neighing and knew that something was wrong.

'I think something's happened to Albert,' said James.

Hearing Albert's name, Black Beauty jerked his head towards the woods and neighed again. James mounted swiftly. 'Take me to him!' he ordered.

Black Beauty obeyed willingly. At least Doctor Gordon understood him; and he carried him swiftly to where Albert had fallen.

The boy had recovered consciousness and was leaning dizzily against a tree. Doctor Gordon made him lie down and examined him for any broken bones or possible concussion. But Albert was a hard headed lad and life as a farm boy had made him strong.

'Duncan—' he mumbled, '– Duncan's a hypnotist!'

In those days hypnosis was regarded with suspicion by most doctors and not many people knew much about it. Doctor Gordon had read one or two articles on the subject but had not taken them very seriously.

'He's hypotised Jenny,' Albert went on. 'That's why she's frightened of Beauty.'

'I don't believe it!'

'To teach you a lesson, he said.'

Doctor Gordon remembered Duncan had mentioned 'methods of treating nervous disorders.' Had he meant that his studies abroad had included hypnotism? His thoughts were interrupted when Black Beauty gave a sudden neigh and disappeared through the trees.

Now that Albert was safe, Black Beauty had a score to settle. Somehow he knew that the young man who had chased Albert out of the Two Foxes needed teaching a lesson.

He galloped into the village just as Duncan was leaving the inn to take up his appointment with old Lady Wainwright. He was about to get into her carriage, smugly aware of the impression he was making, when Black Beauty raced towards him. The powerful horse reared, his nostrils spread wide, and Duncan fell off the carriage step. He scrambled up and tried desperately to get away. The onlookers broke into laughter as Black Beauty chased Mr. Duncan round the village green.

He dodged behind a tree with Black Beauty hot at his heels. Beauty reared again and Duncan scuttled to another tree. And then another, and another, until at last Beauty gave up his game and a tired and bedraggled Duncan sank to his knees crying for mercy.

He was still recovering when Doctor Gordon and Albert reached him.

'Don't let him harm me! Please, Gordon!' cried the hypnotist.

'What about Jenny?' her father demanded angrily. 'Did you stop to think how you were harming her?'

'You slighted me. I wanted to show you that—'

'You've shown me that you're a callous young fool. You're going to undo the damage you've caused.'

Duncan was frightened. He was not sure that he could remove the fear of horses his hypnotic power had planted in Jenny's brain.

In the surgery at York Cottage he managed to put her into a light trance. 'Can you hear me?' Duncan said quietly.

Jenny was breathing deeply; her eyes were closed, and she gave a barely perceptible nod.

'I am going to wake you,' Duncan murmured. 'I shall count from ten – do you understand?'

Again Jenny nodded.

'Your fear of horses will leave you. When you wake, it will have gone completely.'

Duncan began to count. 'Ten . . . your fear is leaving you . . . you are beginning to wake. Nine . . . Eight . . . Beginning to wake . . . Seven . . . Six . . . you are no longer afraid. You are no longer afraid. Five . . . waking now . . . Four . . . Happy and confident . . . Three . . . Nearly awake . . . Two . . . One . . .'

Duncan snapped his fingers and Jenny's eyes flickered

open. She seemed slightly surprised to find everyone looking at her so anxiously.

'How d'you feel?' asked her father.

'Sleepy,' Jenny smiled.

'You need some fresh air.'

'Shall we go outside then?' suggested Amy.

They stood in the stable yard and Albert led Black
Beauty towards them, while Amy and Doctor Gordon
watched Jenny closely. Then slowly she began to walk
forward and gave Beauty a radiant smile of greeting. She
stroked his mane lovingly and Beauty whinnied with
pleasure because he knew his young friend was no longer
afraid of him.

CHAPTER FIVE

THE MEDICINE MAN

It was Arnold Joskins boast that he could sell anything to anyone. His latest commodity was a brightly coloured bottle of water he called Joskins' Universal Panacea; and with his fast and forceful sales talk, he was doing a brisk trade among the more foolish country folk of the district. He was a skinny, quick witted, voluble, tricky rogue, and words poured from him like tap water.

Joskins leant against the whitewashed wall of Mrs. Rogers' cottage in the warm May sunlight, holding a bottle of his medicine and singing its praises.

'Indigestion – liver and kidney troubles – headaches – insomnia—'

'What's that?' asked a rather dazed Mrs. Rogers.

'Sleeplessness, Missis. Sleeplessness,' said Joskins quickly, and resumed his patter. 'Coughs – colds – loss of appetite – why, I've even known it to cure gout. I'm tellin' you Missis – one bottle of Joskins' Universal Panacea in yer house and you'll never have to go to no doctor. Not ever again you won't.'

'How much is it?'

'Sixpence.'

Sixpence was a lot of money in those days, especially for a poor country woman like Mrs. Rogers. She hesitated, wondering if she could really afford a bottle; and Joskins, seeing her indecision, pressed on.

'You can't put a price on good health, Missis. It's the most precious possession you've got. This medicine's an insurance – an investment if you like.'

Mrs. Rogers was just about to buy when Doctor Gordon rode up on Black Beauty and knocked the bottle from the huckster's hand.

'It's coloured water, Mrs. Rogers,' said James angrily, 'but the colouring has lead in it – and it's poisonous!'

Joskins eyes narrowed, and he bared his teeth like a cornered rat. 'Now you wait a minute, matey—' he began.

'No, you wait a minute!' the doctor cut in, losing his temper completely. 'Three of my patients are having terrible sickness because of this rubbish, and if you continue to sell it, I'll see that you're prosecuted!'

'Oh will you? Well just you try it! Because it might bounce back on you. I don't like being told what to do by some nosey village quack!'

James Gordon was blazing with anger; he moved towards Joskins and the man's aggression melted away. 'All right – all right—' he said hastily, running to his little cart, 'I'm goin'.'

'Keep away from Five Oaks!' shouted the doctor.

'Nobody threatens me, matey. Nobody!' retorted Joskins, feeling himself comparatively safe on the driving seat of his cart. The effect of his parting shot was somewhat spoilt, however. For when he flicked the long reins to set his dusty old nag in motion, they snapped and he had to climb down and tie them together while Mrs. Rogers and James chuckled at his embarrassment.

'Very funny, ain't it?' sneered the little man as he scrambled back on to his cart. 'Well, I'll have the laugh on

45

you one day. You see if I don't!' And he rode away muttering revenge.

Albert had taken a holiday job at the saddler's shop in the village. It was a romantic place; a jumble of harnesses, bridles and saddles. Stirrups hung on the walls and leather was everywhere. There were coils of rope, whips, horse brasses and riding boots; there was a great bench and on it lumps of beeswax, long curved needles and balls of thread.

Mr. Surtees owned the little shop. He was an old man with a face nearly as brown as the leather he worked. He had made 'tack' all his life and he prided himself on his craftsmanship. He wore pince-nez and bent low over his work: the years of labour had strained his sight.

He was busy repairing Black Beauty's saddle girth, having lent another saddle to Doctor Gordon for the morning, when he glanced round at Albert. The boy was cutting a long strip from a large piece of leather, his tongue between his teeth as he concentrated on getting it straight. 'You'll bite your tongue clean through, if that knife slips,' muttered Mr. Surtees. Albert put his tongue back in. 'And don't press so hard, Albert,' the old man continued. 'Leather's easy to work with if you treat it gentle.'

Surtees was far from well. He would not admit it but there were times lately when his vision became blurred. He rubbed his eyes. 'Seen my medicine anywhere, Albert?'

Albert found it behind some scraps of leather on the bench. It was a bottle of Joskins' Universal Panacea – and it was nearly empty.

'Is it nasty?' asked Albert as the old saddler took a swig.

'You can hardly taste it.'

Considering it was little more than water this was hardly surprising.

'What d'you take it *for*?' asked Albert.

'Oh, it's just a tonic,' muttered Surtees. 'There ain't nothing wrong with me; fit as a fiddle I am.'

The door of the little shop opened and Arnold Joskins swaggered in. He had recovered from his brush with Doctor Gordon and was as cocky as ever. 'Good mornin' my friend,' he said loftily. 'My blessed reins 'ave snapped. Can you fix 'em for me, eh?'

'You'd better have new 'uns, Mr. Joskins,' said old Surtees.

Joskins grimaced. He didn't want to spend money on a new harness; he was far too mean.

'You can't be too careful. Your life might depend on it,' warned Surtees, giving the girth strap on Black Beauty's saddle a hard tug to test its strength. 'That'll be safe now for Doctor Gordon.'

'Doctor Gordon?'

'Yes. The girth strap broke the other day. It's lucky he wasn't at the gallop, there would have been a nasty accident.'

'Yes,' said Joskins, looking at the saddle. 'I suppose there would . . .'

'Well,' said old Mr. Surtees, sticking his needle into a piece of cork on the bench, 'let's have a look at your harness, Mr. Joskins.'

Joskins was still looking at Black Beauty's saddle. 'D'you mind if I sit down for a bit?' he said, feigning a sudden weariness, 'I've had a bit of a hard mornin'.'

'Certainly – certainly,' said the old man. 'Albert, you'll

47

find some long reins on that shelf over there.'

Albert found the reins and followed Surtees outside. Joskins watched them go, smiling affably, and apparently worn out by his morning's work. But the moment the door shut, he turned swiftly to Black Beauty's saddle. Through the window of the shop, he could see Surtees and Albert examining the worn out harness on his cart. He took a large clasp knife from his pocket, lifted the saddle flap, and began to unpick the stitching with the point of the blade.

Joskins knew what he was doing. He had once worked at a racing stable and had played this evil trick before. His callous act had put a jockey in hospital and won him £50. Now he would be revenged on the meddling Doctor Gordon. The saddle girth would hold until Black Beauty was stretched at full gallop, or taking a jump. Then the girth would break, the saddle would slip, and Doctor Gordon would be thrown.

Joskins smiled to himself as he completed his handiwork, and when Mr. Surtees and Albert returned he was once again sitting quietly.

'All fixed, Mr. Joskins,' said Surtees, throwing the old reins into a waste bin.

'All fixed, eh?' repeated Joskins, relishing the irony of this remark. 'I'm very glad to hear it.'

He had reached the door when Surtees reminded him humbly, he had not yet paid. Joskins apologised profusely for his forgetfulness, but kept moving. 'The thing is I'm a bit short at the moment,' he said glibly, 'but I'll pay you when I call next week.' He reached into the back of the cart and flourished a bottle of Joskins' Universal Panacea. 'A little present,' he said grandly and handed it to Mr.

Surtees. 'No, don't thank me,' he continued hurriedly, preventing Surtees again demanding his money, 'see you next week.'

He raised his hat and the little cart rattled away over the cobblestones. Surtees shook his head ruefully and Albert quivered with indignation. 'Bloomin' nerve!' he said. 'Why won't people pay up straight away, Mr. Surtees?'

'I know someone who will,' replied the old man mildly. 'Get Black Beauty's saddle, Albert. I'll take it now.'

Albert ran back into the shop and picked up the saddle. A good apprentice, he lifted the flap to check that the work was finished. The old man was a bit forgetful these days. He could see at once that something was wrong. Some of the stitches were missing and others were coming undone.

'Hurry up, Albert!' Mr. Surtees called impatiently.

Albert wasn't sure what to say. After all Mr. Surtees was employing him. 'I don't think it's quite finished,' he said finally. 'Some of the stitching at the back—'

'Not finished! Not finished!' Mr. Surtees was furious. 'Of course it's finished! Here, give it to me.'

'But, Mr. Surtees—!'

'I've been repairing saddles all my life,' the old man was trembling indignantly. 'Come on! Hand it over!'

Albert gave him the saddle in silence. Surtees was an obstinate and self-willed old fool, he thought, but there was nothing he could do about it.

'Perfect,' said Surtees, after a quick glance. 'It's perfect. Don't start telling me my job, lad. You're a beginner and you've a lot to learn.'

Albert realised it was impossible to argue.

49

'I want eight more bridle straps cutting before I get back,' called Surtees as he rode off to York Cottage.

Doctor Gordon was pleased to have Black Beauty's proper saddle back but was concerned at old Mr. Surtees' appearance, and also he seemed to have difficulty mounting his horse.

'Are you all right, Mr Surtees?' he asked.

'A bit stiff, that's all,' the old man muttered.

'How's Albert getting on?' asked Kevin.

Surtees smiled in spite of the pain he was feeling. 'He thinks he knows everything!' he said as he trotted away.

Doctor Gordon was extremely busy. His waiting room was full of people suffering from 'Joskins disease' as he called it. He had told them all it was foolish to imagine that a sixpenny bottle of coloured water could cure them of anything. And when they learnt that the so-called medicine was responsible for their stomach pains, they felt very foolish indeed.

The doctor was so busy that Kevin volunteered to deliver some prescriptions. He put the newly repaired saddle on Beauty's back and strapped the girth. 'That's the one you're used to, isn't it?' he said, and Beauty neighed his approval. His old saddle fitted him snugly and was much more comfortable than the borrowed one. Kevin swung himself up and took the haversack from Amy.

'Foster's Farm,' she said. 'D'you know the way?'

'Of course I do,' he replied confidently. 'As a matter of fact, there's a short cut over Wilkes Leap.'

Amy looked worried. 'I think you'd better go the long way round,' she said.

'I wish you wouldn't worry so much, Amy,' said Kevin

somewhat impatiently. 'Beauty's jumped it hundreds of times.'

Albert had not stayed at the shop; he was too worried about the saddle. But while running to York Cottage, he met Mr. Surtees riding to Five Oaks.

The old man dismounted and looked at him suspiciously. 'What are you up to?'

'Nothing,' replied Albert uneasily.

'I told you to get on with your work!'

'Black Beauty's saddle ain't safe, Mr. Surtees!' Albert was beginning to lose his temper.

'Then you'd better tell Doctor Gordon that!' Surtees snapped back at him, 'and a fine fool you'll make of yourself!'

'We'll see!' said Albert, marching past him.

'You'll work for me no longer!'

'That suits me fine!'

Then suddenly Albert saw Kevin galloping across the fields. He called to him but his warning cry was lost in the wind.

How could he stop him? How could he warn him about the weakened saddle girth? There was only one thing he could do. Pushing the angry saddler out of the way, Albert leapt on the man's horse, jumped the hedge and went racing after Kevin. 'You young villain!' shouted Surtees.

Albert knew he had little chance of catching up, for Black Beauty was the fastest horse in the neighbourhood, and even Squire Armstrong's fine hunter, Challenger, could not match him; he also knew that Mr. Surtees' grey mare was well past her prime.

Kevin was enjoying his cross-country gallop. The fresh wind blew in his face, the sun shone, and the blood tingled

In mid-jump, the girth strap split.

in his veins. He glanced back and recognised Albert.

So his friend wanted a race, did he? He'd show him! And he urged Black Beauty to even greater effort, until the horse was going flat out, and the strain was beginning to tell on the weakened girth strap.

Albert grew desperate seeing Kevin going away from him at such a furious pace. If the girth snapped now, the resulting fall could very well break his neck. Yet there was no way to warn him.

He could feel Surtees' mare beginning to tire; and, good rider that he was, Albert knew it would be unfair to ask any more of her. By now he was sure Kevin intended jumping Wilkes Leap and this filled him with dismay. On he rode, praying that his friend would stop his mad gallop and wait for him.

But Kevin kept going – excited and uplifted by Black Beauty's speed. The powerful hooves drummed against the sheep-cropped turf. It was a thrilling sound and Kevin shouted for joy, glancing at the clouds scudding across the sky. He would race them too, he thought; he would race everything that moved; the wild geese, the swiftly running stream, the very wind itself.

Wilkes Leap lay ahead: millions of years ago the limestone layer had slipped, cutting the landscape like a knife for some sixty yards. The drop was over eight feet. A famous highwayman – Nathanial Wilkes – had jumped it to escape his pursuers and so given it a name.

Kevin raced up and Black Beauty sprang into the air. In mid-jump, the girth strap split, the saddle slipped sideways, and Kevin plummeted to the ground.

CHAPTER SIX

BEAUTY'S REVENGE

Albert was still heading for Wilkes Leap when Black Beauty appeared. The horse was without his saddle and Albert knew immediately that he was too late to save Kevin. Anxiously, he followed Beauty around Wilkes Leap to where the boy lay.

Kevin was deathly pale but still breathing, and Albert had the good sense not to try moving him. Instead, he soaked a handkerchief in the nearby stream and placed it gently on his friend's forehead. Then he spoke urgently to Black Beauty. 'You know what's happened, don't you?' he said. 'Get back to the cottage! They'll realise something's wrong when they see you without a saddle.'

Although he did not understand Albert's words, Black Beauty sensed the meaning behind them and knew instinctively he was being asked to get help. He pricked up his ears, gave a reassuring neigh, and went racing off across the fields.

Mr. Surtees had hurried back to York Cottage after Albert had taken his horse. Amy was just saying goodbye to one of Doctor Gordon's patients when the old man shuffled through the gate. 'Miss Winthrop! Miss Winthrop! My horse! He's stolen it!' he gasped.

'Who has?' asked Amy, alarmed to see Surtees so distressed.

54

'Albert!' answered Surtees, fighting hard to get his breath.

'I think you'd better come inside,' said Amy looking at him anxiously.

In the surgery, Mr. Surtees told Doctor Gordon everything that had happened. 'He'd some fool idea that Kevin was in danger—' he said with contempt.

'What sort of danger?' asked James.

'Made me very angry, it did—' the old man muttered, avoiding the question.

'What danger, Mr. Surtees?'

'Well he accused me of bad workmanship,' Surtees was very indignant. 'The young upstart said I'd not repaired Black Beauty's girth proper-like!'

The window of the surgery looked out on the woods and fields, and James suddenly saw Black Beauty galloping riderless, towards the cottage. As the horse drew nearer they all saw that he was without his saddle. And old Surtees began to tremble.

'Which way did Kevin go, Amy?' said James swiftly.

'He took a short cut,' Amy gasped. 'He was going to jump Wilkes Leap.'

Beauty was lathered with sweat by the time James reached his son; the splendid horse had gone flat out to get his master there as fast of he could, and when James dismounted he patted him gratefully. Then the doctor examined Kevin with great care. It was possible the boy had cracked his skull: he was badly concussed, though no bones appeared to be broken. Albert showed James the saddle. 'I told 'im,' he said bitterly. 'I told the silly old fool – but he wouldn't listen.'

The next day, Kevin was still unconscious. Amy refused to leave his room and sat by the bed tending him anxiously. She felt that it was all her fault; if only she had stopped him taking the short cut this might never have happened.

James did his best to reassure her. 'It wasn't your fault, Amy,' he whispered gently as he watched for any change in his son's condition. 'You're not to blame.'

Surtees was convinced that it was *his* fault. He sat at his bench, unable to do any work. Albert had been right after all. Black Beauty's saddle girth had not been completed. Perhaps he was too old, thought Surtees; perhaps his work was becoming slipshod, no longer up to the high standard he had always tried to set. The arms of the Saddlers Company hung outside his shop. He would not disgrace the ancient guild of craftsmen he had belonged to for so many years. He would retire. Surtees sighed and looked fondly at the tools of his trade; at the leather he loved to fashion, and at all the harnesses and saddles he had made. How he would miss the warm smell of his little workroom! The pain twisted his stomach and he was still sipping the patent medicine when Albert came in.

There was a pause. Surtees was embarrassed. 'I didn't think you'd want to come back . . .' he muttered. Then he enquired anxiously – 'How's Kevin?'

'Still unconscious,' said Albert.

Surtees looked out of the dusty window, hardly bearing to face the boy. 'If only I'd listened to you.'

'D'you know why I came back?'

Surtees shook his head.

'Because when people are ill,' said the boy quietly, 'they don't always know what they're doing.'

Surtees said nothing but he looked guiltily at the patent

medicine and tried to hide it behind the balls of thread. But Albert grabbed it from him and held it in front of his face. 'You ain't fooled me, Mr. Surtees. Why don't you go to the doctor instead of dosing yourself with this? It's made a lot of people worse, Doctor Gordon says.'

'I . . . don't like doctors,' said Surtees uneasily. 'They've got some funny ideas . . .'

Albert looked at the old man and realised how afraid he was.

Many people in those days were afraid of doctors and didn't trust them. Doctors might send them to a hospital : and a hospital was a place they dreaded.

'Are you scared to go to the doctor?' asked Albert. Surtees nodded miserably. 'But what if there's another accident?' Albert persisted.

'There won't be any more accidents,' replied the old man sadly.

Then suddenly he remembered Joskins. Had he fixed his harness properly? He could not be sure and he grew agitated and plucked nervously at Albert's jacket. 'Mr. Joskins! Suppose . . . suppose . . .'

Albert had very little time for Joskins but he was anxious to reassure the saddler. 'Don't worry,' he said. 'I'll check his harness. He won't have gone far. But you must promise me that you'll go to see Doctor Gordon.'

Surtees gave Albert his word. Then he apologised for not listening to him the previous day. 'You're a very good friend to me, Albert, I realise that now,' he said.

Albert was very embarrassed by the old man's humility and made his escape as best he could.

He had borrowed Black Beauty again to run errands for Amy and Doctor Gordon, but he felt that it was important

57

to put Surtees' mind at rest, so he set out to find Joskins.

The little trickster had moved away from Five Oaks, and after doing a roaring trade in the small town of Mayberry, was jogging along the open road, feeling very pleased with himself when Albert rode up on Black Beauty.

'What do you want?' said Joskins, eyeing the boy distastefully. He didn't like boys; they often stood at the back of any crowd he managed to gather, making rude remarks and interrupting his patter with catcalls and other rude noises.

'It's about your new harness, Mr. Joskins,' said Albert.

So the old man had sent his apprentice to get the money from him, had he? thought Joskins. Well he was going to be out of luck.

'Clear off! I told 'im I'd pay 'im next week!'

'It's not that,' said Albert. 'There's been an accident ...'

'An accident?' Joskins repeated, his heart suddenly filled with evil triumph. 'Here! Ain't that the Doctor's horse?'

Albert nodded. 'Doctor Gordon ain't been hurt, has he?' Joskins enquired.

'Not him: his son.'

Joskins pretended a vast concern, and put on what he hoped was a suitably grave expression. 'Dear me! What a dreadful thing to 'appen.' This was almost better than he'd hoped for.

'Goin' fast was he?' he asked. 'When it broke?'

Albert looked up at him with a puzzled expression.

'The girth,' Joskins explained.

Albert stared at him. 'I didn't say anything about the girth.'

Joskins cursed his own stupidity. You fool! he thought, you've given yourself away! He tried hard to undo his mistake. 'Oh, didn't you?' he said uneasily. 'Well, in a riding accident—'

'I said an accident, and that's all I said,' retorted Albert, suddenly remembering that Joskins had been left alone in the shop.

He started to turn Black Beauty but Joskins hurled himself from the cart and knocked Albert to the ground. Beauty reared frantically as the boy freed himself from Joskins' grasp and tried to run for it. But the wily man was quick to recapture him. His boney fingers gripped him savagely until Albert gave him a hearty kick on the shin. Joskins howled with pain and let go, and once again Albert ran to Black Beauty. But before he reached him, Joskins caught up and knocked Albert to the ground.

'Help!' shouted Albert at the top of his voice, but Joskins stifled his cries with a dirty hand. Albert bit it furiously and Joskins howled with pain a second time. Then he hauled Albert to his feet and viciously twisted an arm behind his back.

Black Beauty watched the fight; now he came galloping up, trying to get at the stranger molesting his young friend. But Joskins realised the danger and used Albert as a shield against him for he knew Beauty would not harm the boy. Slowly Joskins dragged Albert back to the cart and tied his hands behind him while Black Beauty watched, powerless. He pawed the ground and snorted angrily but he knew that he could not attack Joskins.

'Dangerous brute – ain't he?' said Joskins as he bound Albert's hands. He didn't know what he was going to do with the boy but he couldn't let him get back to Five

59

Oaks. 'You're a bright little lad, ain't yer? Too bright, I reckon,' he hissed.

'What are you going to do?' gasped Albert.

'I ain't decided yet but I'll tell yer one thing, my little squeaker – you ain't goin' to like it. No, you ain't going to like it one bit!'

Albert was forced into the cart while Beauty continued to watch; as it began to move, he charged. Joskins slashed at him with his long whip and Beauty gave a squeal of pain and turned away.

'Keep off!' screamed Joskins and tried hard to make his own horse go faster. Black Beauty wheeled for another attack. He would not give in easily, and the cut from the whip had only served to anger him further. He charged down the hillside neighing his defiance and fury. Then he reared and his hooves thudded against the side of the cart. Joskins slashed wildly with the whip and Beauty turned away again. This time he kept going, and Joskins was very relieved when he saw the horse disappear over the hill.

But Black Beauty had no intention of leaving matters there, and began to follow Joskins at a distance, making sure the man did not see him. When at last the cart stopped by the river, Black Beauty was watching from the wood nearby and waiting for the right moment to act.

Joskins took his tired old nag from the cart and made Albert climb out. He didn't know what to do with the boy. Sooner or later he would have to let him go. Then he would tell everyone how the saddle had been fixed; and if the Gordon kid died Joskins knew he would face a murder charge.

He looked at Albert. 'It's difficult, ain't it?' he muttered.

'Very difficult. I mean I ain't got anything against you personal. But you'd sing like a bird, wouldn't you, if I let you go?'

The only thing he could do was to take Albert to London with him, then he could quietly disappear. He could change his appearance, grow a beard perhaps, and take a new name. By the time the boy had found his way back to Five Oaks, Arnold Joskins would have ceased to exist. Yes, he thought, that was it; then whatever happened he would be safe.

But Black Beauty had other plans for Mr. Joskins. He left his hiding place and charged towards the cart. Joskins, who had been absently whittling a piece of wood with his clasp knife, looked up in horror to see the black horse bearing down on him. Then, as Black Beauty reared, he dropped his knife and fell backwards into the river.

Albert's laughter stopped suddenly when Joskins began screaming in terror that he could not swim. The wretched man's arms clawed wildly at the air. Albert struggled desperately to free himself, watching Joskins with fascinated horror; although he hated and despised the man, he had no wish to see him drown. But his arms had been tied too tightly and he tugged vainly at his bonds. Then he saw the clasp knife: the same clasp knife Joskins had used on Black Beauty's saddle.

Albert lay down quickly by the knife and began to cut himself free. Joskins struggles were growing weaker and it would not be long before he drowned. Albert cut himself in his haste. 'Save me!' choked Joskins desperately. 'Save me!'

At last Albert freed himself. Letting the brake off the

cart, he pushed it straight into the river towards the drowning man. Joskins grabbed at the cart as it floated beside him, and gulped air : he was safe.

The cardboard boxes, each containing a dozen bottles of Joskins Universal Panacea, floated from the back of the cart, spilling their contents into the river. Like a drowned rat, the exhausted Joskins watched his entire stock floating away to sink slowly beneath the surface.

Meanwhile, Mr. Surtees had kept his promise and had gone to Doctor Gordon. He wanted to know how Kevin was, and James did his best to cover up his own worry and reassure the old man.

'Why didn't you come to see me before?' he said when he'd examined him.

'I reckon I'm scared of doctors,' Surtees admitted. 'It was Albert made me come.' He took Joskins patent medicine from his pocket. 'I've been taking this for the last three weeks. Mr. Joskins gave me this bottle yesterday. When he came to have his harness fixed.'

James took the bottle from him. 'And after I'd warned him about selling this muck,' he said grimly.

'Funny that,' Surtees went on. 'Because I'd just finished mending your saddle girth . . .' Surtees dropped his eyes. 'I mean . . . I thought I had . . . It makes me ashamed now, because I told him how a girth giving way can cause an accident.'

'Joskins was in your shop?' asked James, remembering how the man had threatened him.

'Yes. He had a bit of a rest while Albert and me fixed his harness outside.'

James looked grim. So Joskins had meant his threats and Kevin had become the innocent victim! 'I don't think there's much wrong with your memory, Mr. Surtees, or your craftsmanship,' he said.

At this moment, Albert rode up to York Cottage in triumph with Joskins roped to Black Beauty. The wretched man was dripping wet, all his bluster and cockiness washed away by the river. He was still confessing his crime and begging forgiveness, when the window of Kevin's bedroom was flung open.

'He's conscious, Doctor!' beamed Amy. 'And he's going to be all right, I know he is!'

As James ran back into the cottage, Mr. Surtees patted Black Beauty.

'I'm going to make you the finest saddle you've ever seen!' he chuckled.

CHAPTER SEVEN

MISSION OF MERCY

Although Ned had settled down to life in the country and – because he now had Jonah to look after – had lost his fear of horses, he hadn't yet learnt how to ride. Both Kevin and Jenny were quite willing to teach him but he always found some excuse whenever they suggested giving him a lesson. Besides, he thought, he had quite enough to do keeping Jonah out of trouble; for the little pony was often very disobedient. Moreover, Jonah was incredibly greedy and would eat practically anything, until his fat little sides were bulging. Several times Amy had chased him angrily from the kitchen garden where she had found him munching at the runner beans.

Things came to a head one day when Doctor Gordon glanced through the surgery window and saw Jonah busily chewing the large yew bush which grew at the edge of the lawn.

'Shoo! Shoo!' shouted James.

But Jonah wouldn't shoo and continued to eat the yew leaves. So the doctor acted in a very unusual way. He climbed out of the window and grabbed hold of the pony just as Ned appeared on the scene. 'I won't have Jonah wandering into the garden,' said James to the boy. 'He's your responsibility, and if he ate this it could kill him.'

'What is it?' Ned knew very little about plants.

'It's yew,' James explained, 'and it's very dangerous.'

64

'But I thought animals knew all about poisons by instinct,' Ned replied.

Doctor Gordon smiled and shook his head. 'They're a bit like people, Ned. Some are sillier than others.'

The doctor returned to his work and Ned gave Jonah a good talking-to. 'You're always gettin' me into trouble,' he grumbled. 'I don't know why I bother with you, really I don't.' And he led him back to the paddock.

'You keep an eye on him, Beauty,' said Ned as the fine black horse trotted up to them. 'He needs some sense knocking into him.'

He was about to shut the gate when he saw a horseman coming down the lane in a cloud of dust. Both horse and rider were almost done for. As Ned ran across from the paddock, the man pulled up his mount in front of the cottage, jumped to the ground and raced up to the door. He pounded on it frantically until Amy appeared. 'I must see the doctor!' he gasped. 'It's Mary – my poor Mary!'

'What is it, Aunt? What's wrong?' asked Ned after Amy had shown the upset man into the surgery.

'Hush, Ned!' Amy bustled into the kitchen: 'It's no concern of yours.'

'His horse is all foamy!' said Ned.

'Whose horse?' asked Jenny, who was doing the washing up.

'Poor Mr. Danby's,' Amy answered. 'He's galloped over from Catterton, his poor wife's very ill indeed.'

In his excitement and curiosity, at Mr. Danby's dramatic arrival, Ned had forgotten to close the paddock gate. To Jonah such an opportunity was too good to miss, and, despite Black Beauty's attempts to stop him, the little pony slipped out and trotted away to the open fields. Black

Beauty was undecided. Should he follow Jonah or draw the Gordons' attention? He cantered backwards and forwards across the paddock. Then he threw up his head and called to Jonah, but the order to return was ignored and soon the pony was out of sight.

Meanwhile Doctor Gordon was packing his travelling bag. He had to attend Danby's wife as soon as possible; for from what he could learn her life was in danger. 'Get Beauty ready,' he called to Jenny. 'And be as quick as you can!'

Jenny and Ned ran to the paddock just in time to see Black Beauty galloping away. He had decided to go after Jonah by himself, little realising how much he was needed by his master. The children looked at each other with dismay and then Jenny noticed the open gate. Ned looked sheepish. 'I meant to shut it,' he said.

'You meant to!' Jenny said angrily, disgusted by his carelessness. 'Where's Jonah?'

'I was puttin' 'im in when Mr. Danby arrived. D'you think Beauty's gone after 'im?'

Jenny started to run and, a moment later Ned caught up with her. 'Where d'you think you're going?'

'Father wants Beauty now! I've got to find him!'

The cause of all the trouble had reached the fence surrounding Eddington Hall. It was an old fence, badly in need of repair. Here and there, it had been damaged by small boys on apple-scrumping expeditions to Squire Armstrong's orchard. Jonah pushed his way through one of these holes and trotted towards the large formal garden which lay on the south side of Eddington Hall. One of the features of this garden was a splendid colonnade of yew trees.

Black Beauty reached the fence a few minutes later. He could smell Jonah and knew his disobedient little friend lay ahead; but the hole was not big enough for him, so he put his shoulder against the fence and pushed. The weakened and rotten wood collapsed, and he cantered into the park. By the time he reached Jonah, however, the pony had already eaten a stomach full of yew leaves, and when he saw Black Beauty galloping angrily towards him, he trotted off guiltily and attempted to hide. Black Beauty was trying to chase him from the garden when Squire Armstrong appeared.

The Squire almost burst with rage to see Jonah trotting in and out of the flower beds pursued by Black Beauty. He called for help and was soon joined by two grooms, an under-gardener and the bee keeper. They all tried hard to catch Jonah but instead they only added to the damage.

'That wretched man Gordon's to blame for this,' roared Squire Armstrong as Jonah led the chase onto the croquet lawn: 'No sense of responsibility! His children run wild and so do his animals!'

At last, one of the grooms slipped a noose around the tiresome creature's neck, and he was hauled off to the stable and locked away. Black Beauty reared threateningly when he saw this and charged at the Squire, who threw himself to one side, and completely demolished his favourite rose bush. Beauty raced on and wheeled round and round the stable yard calling to Jonah who echoed the cry plaintively. Though the Squire and his men tried hard to catch Beauty, each time they drew near, the angry horse cantered out of range. Finally Beauty sensed that he could not free Jonah so he broke through the men who sought to capture him and sped back the way he'd come.

He charged through the gap in the fence just as Jenny and Ned reached it. Jenny mounted him, and he tried hard to take her back to Jonah but his young rider was firm. 'No, Beauty!' she said. 'Father needs you.'

But Black Beauty didn't want to return to York Cottage. His friend Jonah had been imprisoned, and he wanted to help him. However he had been well trained, and so he finally obeyed Jenny's command.

'What about Jonah?' called Ned as Jenny rode away.

'He's your responsibility,' she threw back at him.

Her father was standing by the empty paddock when she reached home, and never had she seen him so angry. He ordered her to go to her room immediately.

'But father—'

'I asked you to fetch Beauty,' said Doctor Gordon. 'You knew how urgent it was and yet you've been gone nearly an hour gallivanting round the countryside!'

Jenny was almost in tears: 'Father – please listen to me—'

James mounted Black Beauty. 'Mrs Danby is dangerously ill and your behaviour is unforgivable!' Jenny burst into tears as her father rode away. If only he had let her explain. Now it was too late. She ran inside, the tears streaming down her face.

Meanwhile Ned had followed Black Beauty's hoof marks across the park. He looked with dismay at the damage Jonah had gone in the garden; then, keeping under cover, he crept to the long red-bricked stable buildings. There were several grooms tending horses in the cobblestoned yard but no sign of Jonah. Where had they put him? Ned wriggled into the yard and hid behind a water butt. Then he heard a familiar neigh. It was Jonah!

He waited impatiently until all the horses had been led away and the yard was empty, then he quickly unbolted the stall and slipped inside.

Jonah looked at him with lack-lustre eyes, hardly recognising his young master. His mouth was foam-flecked and his coat wet with sweat; and as Ned approached him, his legs crumpled and he fell twitching and gasping on the straw.

'Jonah! Here – what's the matter – eh? Come on, Jonah – it's me!'

Jonah was finding it hard to breathe; his lips were drawn back from his teeth; his eyes were staring, and his sides heaved. Ned knelt down and felt his neck. He was hot, and the muscles twitched under his coat. 'You're burnin' up!' whispered Ned.

But Ned had been seen by one of the grooms. He'd fetched the Squire, and now the two men confronted the boy. 'You were right, Carter!' Armstrong said grimly, 'a two-legged trespasser this time!'

But Ned's concern was for Jonah, and the fact he was trespassing didn't matter to him, nor did he care about being punished as long as something could be done to help his pony.

'He's ill! He's got a fever – look at him.'

Carter knelt down and examined Jonah. 'The boy's right, Squire,' he muttered.

'Then get him out of here,' said Armstrong quickly, 'before any of my horses are infected.'

'But he can't stand, Mr. Armstrong,' Ned argued.

Carter looked closely at Jonah's mouth and drew in his breath sharply. He had found the answer. 'It ain't a disease,' he said softly. 'The little beggars been eating yew leaves.'

'By heaven – I hope you never have another animal to look after,' the Squire muttered angrily to Ned. For a moment the boy looked at them not fully understanding the situation. The Squire was grim-faced; Carter, saddened. Then Ned remembered what had happened at York Cottage and how Doctor Gordon had warned him: eating yew leaves could kill the pony, he had said.

'You know what to do, Carter,' said the Squire.

'You're not going to shoot him!' cried Ned. 'You can't!'

Carter put a hand on the boy's shoulder and did his best to explain. 'He's in pain, you see. It'll be a kindness.'

'But ain't there any way to save 'im?'

'I don't think even a doctor could do much for him now,' said Carter, shaking his head sadly.

A doctor, thought Ned – yes, that was it! He would get Doctor Gordon. Perhaps there was still a chance Jonah's life could be saved. His thoughts were interrupted when Squire Armstrong took hold of him. 'Come on, you've got some explaining to do—'

'Wait! How far's Catterton from here?'

'About three miles. Why?'

'Please, sir,' Ned pleaded, 'give 'im a chance. I'll fetch Doctor Gordon. He can save him – I know he can.'

Now although Squire Armstrong was a bit of a tyrant, he was an honourable man and loved horses. The little Shetland pony had been a great nuisance, and done considerable damage, but Armstrong had no wish to see him die.

'How long do you think he's got?' he said to his groom.

Carter scratched his head. 'Hard to say,' he said. 'Not more than a few hours . . .'

Squire Armstrong turned to Ned; he could see that the boy was very upset. 'All right,' he said, 'I'll give you until five o'clock. But if Gordon doesn't come—' He had no need to finish the sentence.

So Ned set off for Catterton. Already the country air and regular meals were beginning to have a good effect on him, and he was no longer the sickly boy who had begged and thieved his way through the London slums. He ran steadily, nursing his strength. 'Your responsibility,' Jenny had said. Very well, thought Ned grimly, as the sweat began to run down his face, he accepted that responsibility.

He kept on steadily, following each turn of the dusty road, slowing as it led him upwards, gaining speed downhill. Above, the larks sang ceaselessly, almost heartlessly it seemed to him. A rickety farm cart came towards him and the old driver waved cheerfully but Ned barely noticed as he ran past. Trees along the roadside, turned it into a green tunnel, and shaded him briefly from the sun. He passed a signpost. Only a mile to go now! It heartened him to know he would soon be there.

And so, with his head beginning to roll on his shoulders, Ned reached Catterton and asked the way to Mr. Danby's house.

CHAPTER EIGHT

DOCTOR JENNY

Black Beauty stood patiently looking up at the curtained window. He often stood like this waiting for his master to reappear. Sometimes the doctor would look grave, sometimes relieved, and sometimes – when Black Beauty had heard the faint crying of a newborn child – he would walk towards him with a broad smile of happiness on his face. But Beauty was aware that tension surrounded this visit. He could see Danby sitting silently in the garden, his hands clasped and his face pale and drawn.

'She's a little easier,' said Doctor Gordon, coming from the house. 'I don't think she should be moved to the hospital until there's more improvement but it will be all right to see her, though you must keep very calm and only stay for a few moments.'

Danby gave a brief nod and went indoors while James breathed deeply. He was still worried about Mrs. Danby. He walked to Black Beauty and gave the horse an affectionate pat. 'We arrived just in time, Beauty – thanks to you.'

James was sad when he remembered how Jenny had let him down. It was so unlike her; she was usually such a responsible girl. Why had she taken Beauty? It was beyond his understanding.

Beauty's ears twitched and he looked round to see Ned limping up. The boy was tired and his hair hung dankly over his brow. 'What on earth's the matter?' James demanded.

'Jonah's at Eddington Hall,' Ned gasped. 'They say they can't do anything for 'im. He ate some yew . . . It's just like you said – and it's my fault – if only I'd shut that gate—'

'When was this?'

'Didn't Jenny tell you?' said Ned. 'She was so worried – knowing you wanted Beauty urgent like. He went after Jonah, you see.'

'Yes . . . I see,' James replied, thinking of how he'd spoken to Jenny.

'He's dyin' . . . there ain't much time . . . You'll come – won't you?'

James looked from the tearful boy towards the curtained window. He knew he couldn't leave Mrs Danby and hoped Ned would understand. 'No, Ned,' he said quietly, 'I can't come.'

'But . . . if you don't – Jonah'll die!'

'I know,' said the Doctor. 'You see, Ned, we all have our responsibilities, and mine is to Mrs. Danby. If I left her now *she* might die.'

There was a long pause while Ned took in the full meaning of James's words, then he sat down and stared blankly into space. Danby called from his doorway and James moved towards him. 'I'm sorry, Ned,' said James. 'I'm very sorry.'

Ned made no sound but the tears were running down his face; then he ran to James and plucked at his sleeve. 'What medicine would I need for Jonah?' he cried.

'It's no use, Ned.'

'Could Jenny get it ready? Please tell me! I'll get back

to Five Oakes somehow. Jenny can get the medicine – can't she?'

'You'd be too late,' said Doctor Gordon.

The door was slowly shut in Ned's face. Jonah was doomed and there was nothing he or anybody else could do about it.

Black Beauty whinnied softly and trotted over to the distraught figure; he understood the boy was unhappy and wanted to comfort him. He had watched Ned pleading with his master, and had heard Jonah's name; but it was the smell of fear he understood most – the smell of human fear and desperation. He whinnied again and Ned slowly became aware of him. If only he could ride, he thought; if only he had listened to Jenny and Kevin when they had offered to teach him. Black Beauty could carry him swiftly homeward; Jenny could give him the medicine; and he could ride to the stables in time.

'It's no good,' he muttered, 'I don't know how!'

Beauty tossed his head impatiently as if to say : 'I'll teach you. Don't be frightened. You can do it!'

Then the horse turned and presented his flank to the boy, who jumped back, scared by the sudden movement, and stared in fascination at the shining stirrup-iron. Beauty stood very still because he was aware of Ned's fear and he wanted him to be calm. No words were necessary. In some strange way they understood one another. Ned had to mount Beauty, and Beauty waited for him to summon up the necessary courage.

How high the saddle seemed! How wild and powerful was Black Beauty! But with his heart hammering at his ribs, Ned put one foot in the stirrup and tried to haul himself on to the horse. But there seemed to be nothing to get

74

hold of, and he fell back and sat down hard, while Beauty turned and gave him what Ned saw as a look of encouragement. He scrambled up and tried again. And again. By now he was gasping with the effort and no longer timid. Black Beauty stood like a rock and so, abandoning more conventional methods, Ned took a short run and tried to vault into the saddle. But this proved just as unsuccessful.

Ned wouldn't be beaten, for now his blood was up; he led Black Beauty to the fence and by standing on it, at last managed to get into the saddle.

His triumph didn't last long. His feet didn't reach the stirrups and he knew he couldn't ride without them; so, very ungracefully, he dropped to the ground and adjusted the leathers while Beauty waited patiently. Then he used the fence again and gained a feeling of security as he slid his feet into the stirrups.

'All right, Beauty,' he whispered fearfully, 'you're going to 'ave to teach me. And we ain't got much time.'

Beauty trotted off, careful Ned should not be alarmed by the unaccustomed movement. The intelligent animal only began increasing speed when he felt Ned relaxing a little. He could tell the boy was no rider; Ned was sitting all wrong and using the reins as a kind of handle to hang on to, and not as a means of communication.

But they couldn't trot all the way home, so, after a little while, Beauty broke into a canter. This alarmed Ned who thought he would fall. He sawed at the reins just as Beauty expected he would, but the horse kept going. So Ned abandoned his attempt to pull Beauty up and hung on grimly. Soon Beauty was at the gallop and trees and hedgerows became a green blur to his terrified rider. Ned was

Soon Beauty was at the gallop.

jolted backwards and forwards as Beauty lengthened his stride.

A signpost flashed by. It was six miles to Five Oaks. 'We'll never do it!' Ned gasped. But instead of following the track, Beauty veered off and began zigzagging up a rocky hill while Ned shouted to him to stop. 'This ain't the way!' he yelled.

Over the brow of the hill they went and down into the hollow. It was too much for the boy and he tumbled off. Beauty stopped at once and went back to where Ned was getting painfully to his feet and looking around desperately for any landmark that could tell him where he was. They seemed to be miles from anywhere, and he shouted angrily at the horse: 'You fool! You stupid fool! Jonah will die now – thanks to you!'

Beauty whinnied and waited for him to re-mount. 'We're lost! Don't you understand? We're lost!' Ned was in despair, yet somehow he managed to pull himself into the saddle. He tried to turn Black Beauty. But the horse would not obey him. 'It's not the way! We gotta go back to the road!' Ned shouted. It was no use. Stubbornly Beauty cantered on until they reached the river.

Ned slid off and sat down in the blackest despair staring at the water and cursing Beauty for his stupidity. In the distance, a church clock struck four. Ned put his head in his hands, for he was sure now, there was no chance of saving Jonah. They were in the middle of nowhere, an impassible barrier in front of them and time was running out.

Then slowly he raised his head with a puzzled frown. There was something familiar about the distant chimes. What was it?

77

Of course! The bell of Five Oaks Church! It sometimes kept him awake at night.

'We're nearly home!' he said excitedly. 'We can still do it!' And he realised Beauty had known of this short cut all along.

But Ned's elation ebbed away when he looked at the river. There was no bridge within sight. Surely Beauty didn't intend that they should swim across? Yet if Jonah was to survive there was no other way. He heaved himself into the saddle again, took a deep breath to steady his nerves, and urged the horse into the water.

Beauty's plunge nearly unseated him; but he gripped hard with his legs and let the powerful horse do the rest. Although Beauty swam strongly the current carried them some way downstream before they reached the other side. The bank was muddy and this made it very hard for Beauty to get out of the river. Only after several attempts, during which Ned was nearly unseated did he manage to clamber up the bank. Water streamed from his coat and mud splattered from his legs as he galloped homewards. Ned was soaked to the skin and ached in every muscle but his spirits were high, and as they crested the rise, he could see York Cottage and the distant figure of Amy in the garden. He shouted in triumph. 'We done it! We done it!'

Amy and Jenny could hardly believe their eyes when Ned rode up. Swiftly he told them everything. How Beauty had taught him to ride, how he'd taken a short cut, and finally, how they had crossed the river.

'You could have been drowned!' gasped Amy.

'I weren't though,' said Ned who was secretly rather

pleased at the sensation he had created. 'Besides,' he grinned, 'there weren't no bridge!'

Doctor Gordon had several veterinary books because some of his patients brought their sick horses to him; so after careful study Jenny discovered what they should do for Jonah. The book told them little was known about the nature or action of yew poisoning, and that in fatal cases death followed about five hours after eating the plant.

' "For treatment," ' Jenny read ' "we might give two ounces of oil of turpentine in one pint of linseed oil—" '

' "Might give?" ' Ned repeated indignantly, 'don't the feller know?' And he searched in the medicine cabinet for oil of turpentine.

' "To relieve pain, give five grains of morphine hydrochlorate injected hypodermically." ' Jenny closed the book. 'And that's all on yew poisoning.'

Amy bustled off to get the linseed oil from the kitchen while the children found the morphine and the hypodermic syringe. 'Are you sure you know what to do?' Ned asked Jenny anxiously.

'No, I'm not sure!' Jenny flared. Then she controlled herself. 'But I've watched father lots of times and there's no one else to do it.'

They packed everything in a knapsack and Jenny mounted Beauty. 'I'm coming too,' said Ned, though he was worn out, and his clothes were soaked.

'You don't have to,' said Jenny softly, 'you've done so much already.'

Ned smiled wanly. 'Jonah's my responsibility though – ain't he?'

So Jenny pulled him up behind her and, with a wave to Amy, they rode off on their mission of mercy.

At Eddington Hall Carter was looking at his watch when the Squire came into the stable. It was ten minutes to five, 'There's nothing anyone can do for him now,' Armstrong muttered.

'We told the boy, five o'clock, Sir,' said the groom stolidly.

The Squire handed his groom a shotgun. 'You're a sentimental fool, Carter,' he said. Carter sighed and put the gun's muzzle to the suffering animal's head. His finger curled round the trigger . . .

Jenny and Ned ran into the stable and Carter lowered the gun, startled by their sudden intrusion.

'Is your father with you?' asked the Squire.

Jenny stood very still and made herself as tall as she could. When she spoke it was with a grave dignity belying her years and the two men found themselves listening to her almost with respect. 'Doctor Gordon is attending another patient,' she said, 'so I've come in his place. And I know exactly what to do.'

Ned was just as taken aback as the others at the cool calm manner adopted by Jenny. She reminded him very much of Doctor Gordon as she dropped to her knees beside Jonah and began preparing the injection.

It was late that night when Jenny first noticed a change in Jonah's condition. They had gone on with the treatment, refusing to give up hope, and now at last their patient was beginning to recover.

They slept fitfully, taking it in turns to sit with Jonah while Beauty stood guard all night. When dawn came, they knew they had won, for Jonah struggled weakly to his feet and licked their hands gratefully.

Doctor Gordon had spent a similar night with his

human patient – Mrs. Danby. Dozing from time to time, Danby and he had waited for her fever to break. Ned had taken Beauty and James was worried for his safety. He finally left Catterton, satisfied that his patient was out of danger, and a grateful Mr. Danby drove him home.

He found everyone watching Beauty and Jonah in the paddock. Beauty bucked joyfully and Jonah did his little pirouette, while Amy and the children told James the saga of Ned's ride. He was impressed by the boy's courage and determination. Ned had certainly changed in the months he had been with them. James was also proud of his daughter, and of the decisive and cool way she had acted.

CHAPTER NINE

A LONG HARD RUN

It was May, and summer had come quite suddenly. The heavy showers of April had given way to gentler, more settled weather. It was the very best time of the year, Jenny thought, as she left Black Beauty to drink from the old stone trough outside Mr. Surtee's shop, and hurried inside. The old man greeted her cheerfully, and Albert proudly showed her the first bridle he had made entirely by himself. The three of them were still chatting when Jenny happened to glance through the dusty window and saw a girl leap on to Black Beauty and ride away.

'That's my horse!' she cried running out into the street. 'Beauty!' she called. 'Come back!'

In spite of the unknown rider's attempt to urge him onwards, Black Beauty turned and came racing back.

'How dare you take my horse!' cried Jenny.

The girl jumped gracefully to the ground, turned a cartwheel and stared insolently at her. 'You can keep it. I've ridden better donkeys!'

'Black Beauty is a thoroughbred!' Jenny was white with rage.

'Thorough nuisance more like. Go on – take the poor old thing home before it falls over.'

The girl was very pretty but had something of a worldly look. She wore a wide peasant skirt, cossack boots, and an embroidered waistcoat; and she stood, hands on hips waiting for Jenny to make the next move.

'Keep calm, keep calm, my dear miss,' boomed a voice as Jenny stepped forward.

The man who now pushed between the two girls was large and flamboyantly dressed; his fingers sparkled with cheap rings and he wore a huge paste-stud in his cravat. A cheroot stuck out from his fleshy lips and now he removed it with an elaborate gesture and flicked away the ash. 'My daughter's the finest rider in Europe,' he announced grandly.

Jenny controlled herself with an effort. 'I want to know why she took my horse.'

Several passers-by had seen the row develop and now watched curiously. Police Constable Dickens elbowed his way through them. 'All right! All right! Now what's all this about?'

The portly figure bowed. 'A trivial misunderstanding, officer,' he boomed, 'nothing more. My daughter here – full of spirit – no harm intended – merely a harmless jape – Come – Dolly me girl – apologise. Apologise to the young lady.'

'I'm sorry.' The girl was very unconvincing.

Police Constable Dickens looked the man up and down. 'And who might you be, sir?' he said, as a crowd began to collect.

This was just the question the stranger had been waiting for. He had achieved his first aim, and drawn a crowd, and now he launched into a speech, climbing on to some bales of straw in order to be seen clearly by everyone.

'Who *might* I be?' he repeated ironically, sticking his thumbs in his waistcoat. 'Well, now – I *might* be the Emperor of China. But I ain't. I *might* be the King of

Egypt – but I ain't. I am – *in fact* – that unique impressario – that fairground magnifico – that showman extraordinary—' and here he again bowed low, and swept off his hat – 'J. Otis Waygood.'

The little crowd gave him a polite round of applause. Somehow it seemed expected of them. Police Constable Dickens wasn't really sure how to cope with the situation.

'Tonight, ladies and gentlemen,' J. Otis Waygood continued, 'I shall provide you with a positive feast of entertainment – culminating in a most amazing display of equestrian skill' – he quickly singled out the most stupid-looking amongst his listeners – 'trick riding to you, Sir!' The crowd laughed. 'This educational demonstration will be given by my daughter.' The showman took a money bag from his pocket and jingled it hastily when he saw one or two people start to drift away. The sound of the money stopped them as Waygood knew it would. But P.C. Dickens, realising the man was some kind of mountebank, tapped his arm and asked him to move on.

'Two minutes, officer,' Waygood pleaded. Dickens relented. No harm in two minutes, he thought.

'In this bag my friends – are twenty-five golden sovereigns – waiting for anyone able to out-ride my daughter in a race to be run this afternoon at three o'clock. The entrance fee is a mere two sovereigns, ladies and gentlemen.'

Jenny, who had been excited by the possibility of paying Dolly back by winning the race now looked glum. She couldn't afford to enter.

'Come now – surely someone will accept the challenge,' mocked Waygood, 'or are you afraid to race against a mere slip of a girl?'

This riled the more adventurous spirits in the crowd and several men came forward. Now Dickens was in a real pickle. Somehow things had been taken out of his hands: it looked as if the race was going to happen.

'Who else is prepared to pit his skill against my daughter? I warn you gentlemen – she's fast – oh yes – she's very fast indeed!'

Jenny trotted off down the street to collect her father's watch from Mr. Hilton's shop. If only she had two sovereigns she would show Dolly Waygood no horse could beat Black Beauty. Her frustration turned to dismay however when Mr. Hilton gave her back the watch saying it was no longer worth trying to repair it. 'I'm afraid he's worn out,' he said, as if the watch was some old gentleman about to die. 'Been a good old feller though,' he added with a smile.

James was sad when Jenny returned it to him. It had been in his family for many years; it had belonged to his father and to his grandfather. He was going to be lost without it, and, at the moment, he couldn't afford another. He put it away in the drawer of his desk while Jenny babbled on about the race. 'I've got the sovereign you gave me at Christmas, and you'd only have to *lend* me another.'

James told her that on no account would he let Black Beauty be raced. Besides, the idea of throwing away two sovereigns on such a harebrained venture was ridiculous. Jenny knew she couldn't persuade him to change his mind, so she went to the kitchen and unburdened her heart to Amy.

'Father doesn't understand,' she said unhappily.

'I'm sure he does,' Amy replied. 'Besides, two sovereigns is a great deal of money.'

85

'But I'll get them back when I win – and twenty-five more as well. I could buy a lovely watch then.'

'A watch?' questioned Amy.

'Yes. Father's can't be repaired, you see. That's why I want to win the race. That and another reason. I know how much he needs one, and he can't afford it – he simply can't.'

Amy put the apple pie she'd just made into the oven and straightened up, wiping her hands on her apron. 'Suppose you didn't win?' she said.

The idea had never occurred to Jenny. She was quite sure she would win; after all, she would be riding Black Beauty. Besides, she had such good reasons for winning; to teach Dolly Waygood a lesson, and replace her father's watch. Amy sighed, touched to see the confidence shining in the girl's eyes. 'It could be dangerous,' she said softly.

'Not with Beauty,' came the swift reply.

Amy was very thoughtful as Jenny helped her scrub down the kitchen table. Perhaps she ought to play fairy godmother to the girl's Cinderella. The only magic needed was a single sovereign. She paused in her work and spoke quietly. 'Could you fetch the money box from my dressing table, Jenny?'

For a moment Jenny didn't grasp the full meaning of Amy's words; then she rushed into her arms, and hugged her gratefully, too overcome to speak.

Meanwhile, J. Otis Waygood, well pleased with the outcome of his morning's work, was sitting idly on the steps of his caravan playing 'A Little of What you Fancy Does You Good' on his concertina. Money was what he fancied, and he fancied more than a little. So far there were twelve entries for the Waygood Stakes that afternoon, which made twenty-four more sovereigns for him. Nearby, Dolly was feeding her two splendid Arab stallions. They were fiery creatures – so alike they might have been twins.

The Waygoods had pitched their caravan on the village green opposite The Two Foxes, and from time to time curious villagers strolled across and gawped at them. When Ned – homeward bound from a fishing expedition – saw the caravan, he too, went for a closer look.

His face dropped when he recognised Waygood, for he'd known him in London in the bad old days and was well aware that the man was a very tricky customer.

Ned wanted to find out what J. Otis Waygood was getting up to in Five Oaks, so he hid nearby. Presently, Squire Armstrong rode up on Challenger. 'What's this race about, my man?' he said.

Waygood finished his song and put the concertina down carefully, then he bowed deeply. 'Whom do I have the honour of addressing?'

'My name's Armstrong,' the Squire answered coldly. 'I own most of the land around here, and if you attempt to run this ridiculous steeplechase of yours, I'll see you'll do some running yourself; and you won't stop till you're out of the county.' Then he wheeled his horse and would have ridden off had not Waygood run after him.

'One moment – one moment my dear sir—' he said, mopping his brow with a large spotted handkerchief, '— I beg you – please reconsider – I appeal to you as a sportsman, sir—'

'Sportsman?' sneered the Squire. 'The rag tag and bobtail of the village careering over my land!'

Waygood smiled oilily up at him rubbing his hands

87

deferentially. 'I have been most careful – most careful in choosing the course—' he turned to his daughter, 'ain't I, Dolly, me girl?'

Dolly dropped the Squire a demure curtsey. 'Oh, yes, he has, your Honour – ever so careful.'

Waygood fumbled in his pockets and produced a grubby piece of paper which he flapped at Armstrong, now beginning to be amused by the man's eagerness to please him.

'I have here, a rough map—' said Waygood, handing it up to the Squire. 'I realise the error I have committed in not first obtaining your permission,' he apologised.

Armstrong studied the map. He could see it would be a very interesting and difficult race. 'By heaven it's a long hard run . . .'

'And against my daughter, sir . . .'

Armstrong looked at Dolly who stared back bold as brass.

'She's only a young thing, sir, but a most brilliant rider. Unbeatable,' said the showman.

'Unbeatable – eh?' repeated Armstrong, glaring at the insolent girl. 'Yes,' said Dolly conceitedly. 'Unbeatable.'

Now the Squire was not used to disrespect – especially from vagabonds living in caravans – and he was stung by Dolly's forward manner. 'You're too sure of yourself, my girl,' he said.

'Oh, am I?' mocked Dolly.

'I've a mind to teach you a lesson.'

'You might be the one to learn, sir.'

Armstrong was furious. The hussy was making a fool of him. 'Fifty gold sovereigns I can beat her by half a mile,' he said to Waygood, who made a pretence of being frightened by such a large wager, though secretly he was delighted. 'Accept or I'll have the race called off,' said the Squire.

Waygood acted as if cornered and stammered a scared acceptance, then as he watched the Squire ride away he winked at Dolly. 'Well – me girl – we'll be in the money this afternoon – with *extra* thanks to that fool!'

'Really fell for it – didn't he?' laughed Dolly.

Waygood sat heavily on the steps, picked up his concertina and began to play softly. 'I'm proud of you, Dolly,' he said. 'Real proud.'

'Are you sure the tricks will work, Pa?'

'Come inside and I'll show you.'

These last remarks only confirmed Ned's suspicion, and now he was certain that the Waygoods' race would be 'fixed'. As yet, however, he had no proof, so he waited till the door of the caravan was closed and then crept up the steps to listen at the keyhole. Waygood was talking earnestly to his daughter and the words came clearly to Ned.

'. . . after that – no one'll catch you. But just in case – just in case, Dolly, I'm rigging a trip wire in the woods. Just here – see?'

Ned was horrified. If only he could see the map. Then Dolly's voice answered her father's. She was worried about the trip wire, and was against it. 'It could break a horse's leg,' Ned heard her say.

But Waygood swept her objection aside impatiently. 'With the bets I've taken already, this race is worth a great deal of money, and I can't afford to take any chances. You are going to win and I don't give a fig how you do it—'

Waygood broke off and listened. There was someone outside, he was sure, for he'd heard the steps creak as Ned moved slightly. Despite his size, Waygood was surprisingly quick on his feet. He pulled the door open and Ned stumbled into the caravan and fell at his feet. Waygood hauled him up and pushed the door shut.

There was something very familiar about this eavesdropper. Where in the world had he seen him before? Then Dolly remembered. 'It's Ned!' she gasped. 'Ned Lewis!'

'Well, well, well! I never expected to find you in the country, Ned me boy,' breathed Waygood – holding Ned down while Dolly tied him to a chair – 'funny place to find a boy like you – or are you a reformed character these days?'

'I don't know about that,' Ned retorted, 'but you ain't changed yer tune 'ave you?'

'True – true,' admitted Waygood. 'The same tune perhaps – but a very different . . . "*fiddle*".' And he giggled at his joke while Dolly finished her work.

'I'll tell 'em all you've fixed the race.'

'But you'll 'ave no proof, Ned me boy, will you?' replied Waygood picking up the map and slowly tearing it into little pieces, 'no proof at all . . .'

'All right,' said Ned, 'but please don't use that trip wire! For the sake of the horses!'

'I think I shall cry in a minute,' Waygood jeered, 'I really shall.'

But Ned's plea had once again pricked Dolly's conscience, so her father was forced to speak sharply to her thus preventing any further argument about the trip wire.

'Gag him!' he ordered.

CHAPTER TEN

WAYGOOD'S TRICKS

The sun shone gaily that afternoon, and the whole village turned out for the race. By two o'clock, the village green was crowded with spectators excitedly discussing the different riders' chances; while, from outlying farms, people continued to arrive, some in little two-wheeled traps, others – with large families – in heavy wooden carts; until the green looked as if a fair was being held. Indeed, there was a carnival spirit in the air: a holiday mood seemed to grip everyone, and the landlord of the Two Foxes rubbed his hands gleefully when he saw how thirsty the impending steeplechase had made his patrons.

Yet amid all this hustle and bustle, Dolly Waygood appeared cool, calm and collected. She sat motionless on one of her Arabs, and no one seemed to have noticed that the other one was missing. Dolly's lip curled with contempt at the gaping country folk and she thought what gullible fools they were.

There was a cheer from the crowd as Squire Armstrong rode up on Challenger, and cantered to the starting line. Dolly noticed the horse was fresh and full of spirit but she smiled to herself, confidently. Her father would make it impossible for anyone to beat her. The rest of the opposition she dismissed out of hand. They were strong, useful hunters, no doubt, but even had the race been a fair one she knew she could beat them easily. However, when

Jenny trotted up on Black Beauty, Dolly's eyes narrowed. Her scathing remarks about him, that morning, had been made deliberately, to create a scene and draw a crowd, but even the short ride down the village street had been long enough to tell her that Black Beauty was something rather special.

Police Constable Dickens was there, rather flustered and surprised by the swift turn of events. The Squire rode over to him. 'Where's Waygood?'

'Gone ahead, Mr. Armstrong,' the policeman replied. 'To see nobody cuts any corners.'

Jenny was impatient for the race to start. She didn't want her father to arrive and stop her taking part. In silence she handed her two sovereigns to Dolly who pocketed them with a sneer. Jenny's heart was beating wildly, it was one thing to dream of winning but quite another to actually do it. This was real : she had to prove herself with Beauty's help, so she gripped the reins nervously and trotted to the starting line.

It was some time before P.C. Dickens – cunningly recruited by Waygood – could start the race; for the horses sensed the excitement of the occasion, and the crowd pressing forward upset them and made them jostle and turn away, while their riders swore and shouted. Only three horses stood their ground : Dolly Waygood's pale Arab, Squire Armstrong's Challenger, and Black Beauty. Several times the line would form only to break again, as a cursing rider was forced to turn away, but at last all was ready, the signal given, and off they went amid a great roar from the crowd.

In the split second before P.C. Dickens dropped his flag, Jenny's nervousness betrayed her, and she twitched at the reins. Black Beauty – confused by this mistake – checked in mid-stride and was slow to get away. By the time he'd recovered, the rest of the field were well clear. Races, however, are not won at the starting post, and though Jenny knew this she continued to blame herself bitterly as Beauty thundered after the others.

Dolly Waygood got away very fast indeed. Her splendid mount moved effortlessly, well suited to the firm going. The Arab liked to be in front and this helped Waygood's plan. The showman had been careful to avoid any areas of heavy peaty soil, for this would have tired the Arab quickly and cut down his speed. The land around Five Oaks was ideal and he began to increase his pace.

But Challenger kept up with him. The Squire spurred him on, with grim determination. He saw Dolly glance back, and could tell she was rattled to see he'd kept up with her. But she was still in the lead as the field stormed towards the first jump and poured over it in a flashing blur of boots and flying manes. For an instant the horses seemed to become a great wave rolling over the jump. The wave crashed down, broke, and as if by magic, turned back into galloping horses again.

Two riders had been thrown and they crouched down as Black Beauty – the last to jump – landed lightly between them and raced on. He had a lot of ground to make up and Jenny whispered fiercely to him: 'We can do it – we can do it Beauty! *And we must*!'

J. Otis Waygood was watching the race through a telescope, from the top of Marne Hill. Dolly was flying along the valley, well clear of the following group led by Squire Armstrong. He put the telescope away and trotted down the other side of the hill to prepare the first of his little surprises. Waygood had worked out the course very carefully. Here, it led down a narrow lane with ditches and hedges on either side, the perfect place for an ambush. A flock of sheep grazed in a field to one side of this lane and Waygood waited by the gate for his daughter. As Dolly flashed by, he drove the sheep into the lane and galloped away unseen.

Squire Armstrong was the first to see the sheep blocking the lane ahead. A keen huntsman, he had developed the ability to think and act quickly in an emergency, and so, without losing speed he set Challenger at the hedge and jumped it magnificently. Then he raced past the sheep and jumped back into the lane again.

Only one other rider reacted with the same quickness and skill. While the rest of the field milled among the sheep, their horses plunging and rearing in noisy confusion, Jenny Gordon jumped Black Beauty into the field and out again, just as the Squire had done!

All this time, Ned had been trying to free himself. Finally, he rocked to and fro until his chair crashed to the floor. Its back, weakened by years supporting Waygood's fat body, broke off and Ned was able to get free. The locked door was too strong to force, so he hurled a stool through the window and climbed out. He searched vainly in the crowd for P.C. Dickens; but the constable had been called to break up a fight in the Two Foxes and – the excitement over – was engaged in the dull business of taking everyone's name. So Ned ran to Marne Hill. He knew Waygood would be there, for he'd heard him tell Dolly so. Somehow he had to stop him using the trip wire.

Meanwhile, unable to find either his horse or his

daughter, Doctor Gordon had been staggered to learn from Amy that not only had Jenny entered the race but had actually done so with Amy's help.

'Your irresponsibility staggers me, Miss Winthrop,' he exclaimed angrily, as they confronted one another in the kitchen.

Amy hadn't been called 'Miss Winthrop' by the doctor for years, and she flared back at him. 'Don't be so – so pompous, *Doctor* Gordon!' she retorted indignantly.

'Pompous!' James couldn't believe his ears.

'Yes – pompous!' Amy repeated, completely losing her temper. 'Pompous and tyrannical!'

The cause of this noisy row was careering downhill hot in pursuit of Squire Armstrong. Black Beauty was going well, he had great staying power, but also he had that rare quality which often means the difference between a fine horse and a champion – the quality of courage. Jenny could feel it as he tore along, overhauling Challenger stride by stride. Beauty never spared himself, he always gave of his best; and though an animal, he possessed true heroism and nobility.

Jenny saw Armstrong rise at the jump ahead and prepared herself. As Challenger landed, Black Beauty took off, and, high in the air, drew his hind feet up sharply and sailed over cleanly to land rock-steady and ready for more.

Dolly was worried. The margin of her lead was narrowing. There were only two horses behind her but they were the two she feared most. She had to reach her father for the Arab was tiring fast. On she dashed to the wood ahead.

Waygood was waiting with her other horse, fresh and

eager to be away. Dolly galloped up, leapt on its back and was off again before her father had finished pulling the spent horse into hiding. This was the reason the two Arabs were so alike. But he was only just in time. Armstrong, hotly pursued by Jenny, hurtled past, and Waygood mopped his brow. They were too close for his liking. He had to get to the trip wire and he hoped that Dolly would have time to pull off the next trick he'd prepared. If not, he thought grimly, he would be ready at the trip wire.

About a quarter of a mile ahead, the course led through an open gate. From this gate a hedge ran uphill, concealing a farm wagon held back by a cunningly placed rope. Once the rope was cut, the cart would roll forward, blocking the gateway.

The Squire and Jenny were neck and neck and only about fifteen yards behind, when Dolly shot the gate, leant from her saddle and slashed through the rope with a sharp knife.

Jenny and Beauty passed the Squire and had nearly reached the gateway, when the heavy cart rolled across in front of them.

It was as if a wall had suddenly appeared and it seemed that they must be smashed against it. Beauty was at full gallop, yet instinctively he leapt upwards.

Time slowed down. To jump the cart was impossible. Jenny was sure of this. Everything became unreal. They were still going upwards. Jenny found herself looking into the cart. She could see a rusty bucket. And a sickle. Some sacks. A broken spade. Beauty continued to rise, and now Jenny could see over the cart to the ground the other side. The dreamlike detachment continued. The cart passed

96

The cart passed under them.

under them. And the ground seemed to float up to meet them. All this happened in the second that passed as the Squire's horse slithered to a halt inches away from the cart. Afterwards, whenever the Squire attempted to tell friends about Black Beauty's great jump he would break off, finding words inadequate, and simply say: 'You should have been there! You should have been there!'

The landing jarred Jenny from her trance-like terror. She thought Beauty was going to fall but by some miracle he kept his feet and galloped on. He's done the impossible, thought Jenny. Nothing could stop them winning now!

Dolly looked back, staggered to find Black Beauty still behind her. She raced along the valley for the second time while Waygood watched anxiously. He ran into the wood where the trip wire lay across the path of the oncoming horses. He could hear them in the distance, the muffled drumming of their hooves growing louder. Then Dolly was thundering down the path towards him and, behind her, the girl on the splendid black horse!

With his daughter safely over the trip wire, he pulled it taut and tied it off swiftly round a tree.

But Beauty saw the sunlight glinting on the wire and pulled up suddenly. He had once jumped into wire and had never forgotten it.

Jenny, unprepared for Beauty's abrupt halt, went crashing to the ground. Waygood coiled the trip wire and waddled to his horse very pleased with himself. The race was won, passing the finishing post, a mere formality.

But J. Otis Waygood had reckoned without Ned. The boy was toiling up the hill when Dolly came out of the wood. Startled by his sudden appearance – for she'd left him tied up in the caravan – her concentration wavered. At that instant her horse stumbled and she was thrown.

But Ned was more concerned about the trip wire. He ran past her into the wood and came face to face with Waygood.

He ducked off the path and pushed his way into the tangled undergrowth. But the wily showman dismounted and charged in after him, puffing and blowing like an old steam engine. Ned knew the woods well and led him a mazey dance through the thickets, until Waygood, fat belly heaving under the gaudy waistcoat, had lost all sense of direction. Then Ned left him and crashed his way back to the path; he had heard Black Beauty neighing in the distance.

Jenny had been lucky, she had fallen well and had been merely winded. Now she wept bitterly. 'We could have won, Beauty! We could have beaten her!'

'You still can!' cried Ned, running up, 'Dolly's fallen too! Go on! Go on!'

Jenny threw herself on Beauty and urged him to the gallop and almost ran down Waygood as he came stumbling back.

Dolly was still dazed when she reached her. Jenny could have ridden on to win, but she was a doctor's daughter, and she pulled up and went to the girl.

'Are you all right?' she asked. Dolly couldn't understand. Why hadn't Jenny gone on to victory?

'There's a mile still to run,' said Jenny helping her to her feet.

Dolly found it hard to believe. Despite all the tricks played on her, this girl wanted to win fairly. The showman's daughter felt very ashamed. Win or lose, she vowed that from now on, her life would be very different. Then they lined up their horses and after a signal from Jenny, careered off down the long hill to the village.

Ned watched them go from the wood's edge. 'A joke – that was all, Ned me boy – just a joke!' babbled Waygood behind him.

'Tell that to the village!' Ned shouted back at him, beginning to run downhill. 'And the Squire!'

The two horses were neck and neck as they finished their descent and began the flat run to the village. Three jumps remained.

Over the first they flew with Dolly's horse just ahead. 'Come on Beauty!' yelled Jenny. The second hedge loomed up and over they went; this time Beauty's jump landing him ahead of the Arab. They could see the village green clearly now and heard a great shout go up from the crowd.

They cleared the final jump together. Beauty had run twice the distance of the other horse and had brought off the mightiest leap of his life. But now his courage – the courage of a champion – began to take him ahead. The sight broke the Arab's spirit and Dolly knew she had lost.

And so, her eyes shining with triumph, Jenny Gordon swept past the winning post on Black Beauty.

The crowd surged forward cheering wildly as she slid from the saddle and pressed her head against Beauty's neck. She knew she would never forget this moment; it would remain in her memory for ever. A sea of hands stretched out to shake hers. 'Well done, lass! Well done!' The tumult was deafening. Through it all Black Beauty stood, his sides heaving, the steam rising from him, as he sucked in great draughts of air through his spread nostrils.

The crowd parted. It was Dolly. 'You won,' she said. 'And you won fair and square.'

'I was riding Black Beauty,' Jenny replied, as if that explained everything.

But Jenny's triumph was short-lived. Doctor Gordon elbowed his way through the crowd and took her back to York Cottage in silence.

The scene in his study was a painful one. It was the most severe dressing-down the Doctor had ever given her and when he finished speaking Jenny crept to bed feeling very ashamed.

For the next week she slaved in the house. James organised what seemed like an unending list of tasks for her. She beat the carpets until the dust choked her. She scrubbed the kitchen floor, and polished the stair rails, until she thought her arms would drop from their sockets. She darned vast piles of socks, she ironed and mended, she washed and cleaned, until her hands were raw.

Then, one day, a small parcel arrived for James, and the writing on it was familiar. Inside was a beautiful watch and though there was no message, James knew who it was from.

Outside in the garden, he could hear the steady thump of the carpet beater.

When he reached Jenny, he stopped her working and held out the watch. 'You won that race for this, didn't you?' he said gently.

Jenny smiled at her father. 'Well,' she said, wiping her hot and mucky face on her sleeve, 'it was Beauty who won the race, really. But it *was* my idea!'

CHAPTER ELEVEN

THE ESCAPE

To begin with, it was all Black Beauty's fault. If he'd turned for home when he'd trotted from the daisy-covered field, Kevin and Albert would never have seen her.

'Don't be silly,' muttered Kevin. 'Home's this way.' Then both he and Albert gaped. A girl was running towards them down the tree-lined lane.

She was young, with long fair hair streaming behind her, and her face was very pale. As she came nearer they saw that she was weeping. Her eyes were hunted and panic-stricken, and when at last she noticed the boys she cried out for help.

She reached them, exhausted and sobbing; then she began to sway, and Kevin – fearing she was going to faint – caught hold of her. 'What is it?' he asked urgently. 'What's wrong?'

She seemed too terrified to speak but instead pointed down the road, trembling violently. As she did this, a carriage appeared in the distance. With a moan of despair, she broke from Kevin and tried to run but he quickly caught up with her.

The carriage rattled up and stopped. Everything about it reminded them of a funeral. It was shiny black; as shiny and as black as the tall top hat of its driver. The horses were black, their harness, black; even the upholstery was black. And sitting, dressed all in black, bolt upright like two undertakers, were the grim-faced occupants of the carriage – a man and a woman. Both of them were tall and thin, and they stared straight ahead, reminding Kevin of two ravens he'd once seen frozen to death on a fallen tree.

'Get her!' The whiplash command rang out sharply and the blue-chinned driver jumped down and hurried the protesting girl back to the carriage. 'No! No! Let me go!' she begged him.

The couple in the carriage continued staring straight ahead. They could have been a pair of tailor's dummies. They never moved, or gave any sign they were alive, and when the girl was bundled in beside them, it was as if she didn't exist.

Albert dismounted. He was very angry. 'Here – you can't do that!' he cried.

Once again the girl was weeping, her face in her hands. The coachman turned the carriage. 'Just a moment, you!' shouted Kevin as it began moving off.

'Stop! Are you deaf! Stop I say!' yelled Albert; but the wheels turned faster and soon the two boys were left alone.

The sound of the carriage died away in the distance. For a moment Kevin and Albert stood motionless, hardly believing what they'd seen. It was like something out of one of Jenny's romantic novels. The incident had been melodramatic and bizarre. Who was the girl, and who were the strange pair who'd driven off with her? Kevin and Albert had to find out.

They mounted Black Beauty and cantered down the road after the carriage. About two miles further on, a drive led off down a long avenue of elms.

'Well, they couldn't have gone that way,' muttered Kevin, 'it leads to Granley Hall.'

Both of them knew that Granley Hall had been empty for many years; but Albert's sharp eyes noticed the fresh tracks made by a pair of horses and the sharply marked wheel-ruts of the carriage. 'Well, it may have been empty,' he said, 'but if you ask me, there's somebody living there now!'

They followed the tracks until a high and rusty pair of gates barred their way. Trees hung low over the lane and the whole place was surrounded by an atmosphere of gloom. Ivy wound its way up the decaying ironwork, and it seemed unlikely the gates had been opened at all recently. Then the boys caught sight of a shining new padlock and chain, so they dismounted to examine it.

The garden was very overgrown, yet they could see through the gate that the tracks led onwards to the distant house, half hidden by giant rhododendrons. A high wall ringed the place and the boys led Black Beauty round it until they judged that they were somewhere near the back of the house. Albert was getting nervous and half-heartedly suggested going home: they were already late and Doctor Gordon was waiting for Black Beauty.

Presently, they came to a recently bricked-up doorway. 'That's new as well,' whispered Kevin. 'They've made sure no one's getting in!'

'Or ... *out*!' Albert added dramatically.

Kevin looked at the high wall. Albert could see what was in his mind. 'Come on, Kevin,' he said. 'We'd better get back. I mean, there ain't nothing we can do – is there?'

'Hold Black Beauty still,' said Kevin, mounting and slowly standing upright on the saddle, using the wall to balance himself. He peered over into the garden and gasped with surprise. The lawn was smooth as green velvet, and fresh flowerbeds had been planted. The bushes had been pruned and shaped, the greenhouse freshly painted and the little fountain in the lily pond played merrily. It was all very different from the overgrown driveway with its ivy-covered gates.

There was no one in the garden or on the distant terrace and Kevin whispered this information down to Albert. Then he began to climb over the wall.

'Kevin!' hissed Albert. 'What d'you think you're doing?'

'That girl's in trouble!'

'So will you be if you climb over that wall.'

'You stay here!' said Kevin as he disappeared.

'He's gone soft in the head, Beauty!' said Albert. 'He's gone completely off his nut!'

Kevin moved very cautiously, using the thick bushes to cover his approach, until he was quite close to the house. He reached the corner of one of the outbuildings and saw that to get any closer he must cross open ground. He peered round the building, and, to his horror, saw the burly figure who'd driven the carriage, walking briskly towards his hiding place. Just when it seemed the man couldn't fail to see him, there was a shout from the distance. 'Evans!'

Kevin had heard that voice before. It had the same cutting sound. The coachman stopped and began retracing his steps. 'If you ever forget to chain those gates again, I'll dismiss you on the instant,' Kevin heard his master say.

The two men turned away enabling him to cross the

gap and hide again. He was now close to the conservatory, a green jungle of exotic ferns, with marble statues standing on the tiled floor.

In the middle of the conservatory stood the girl, her head bowed. The black-clad woman was addressing her: '—and when he returns, you will be severely punished for such wicked disobedience.' She gathered up her skirts and swept into the main part of the house, leaving the girl still motionless.

Kevin tapped on the glass. He didn't want to frighten her and gave her an encouraging smile. She recognised him instantly and gestured for him to enter.

'How did you get in?' she whispered.

'Over the wall—' Kevin began but broke off when he heard voices.

The girl looked frightened. 'You must go,' she whispered. 'If they find you here—'

'But what's going on? Why are you—?' The voices were coming nearer.

'Please!—' the girl pleaded.

Kevin was very close to her as her blue eyes began to brim with tears. 'What's your name?' he said gently.

The girl shook her head. 'He's coming!' she whispered urgently.

'Cicely!' called a cruel voice Kevin recognised.

He smiled down at her. 'Cicely,' he repeated softly. Kevin slipped from the conservatory with only seconds to spare.

Cicely's tormentor gripped her arm cruelly and thrust her back into the house. There was nothing Kevin could do but return to Albert, by now very worried his friend had been caught. As they rode away from Granley Hall, Kevin vowed he would solve the mystery.

'You're very naughty boys to be so late,' said Amy angrily, back at the cottage. 'Doctor Gordon's been waiting for Black Beauty nearly an hour.' They tried to tell her all about their adventure but Amy thought they were about to begin a long and unlikely excuse – as they so often did – and refused to listen.

'Father,' Kevin persisted, as James mounted Black Beauty, 'there's people at Granley Hall. They're holding a girl prisoner there.'

'Nonsense!' said the Doctor, who was angry with the boys for delaying him.

Kevin tried again but his father cut in. 'I'm late,' he said and rode away.

'Late for what?' asked Kevin. 'Where's he going?'

Amy turned at the cottage door. 'Granley Hall,' she said.

Doctor Gordon had been invited to tea at Granley Hall to meet the new residents, Joshua Eglington and his sister Edith. Squire Armstrong was there and so was the vicar, the Reverend Grout. They all sat rather stiffly drinking weak tea from delicate china while Edith Eglington handed round tiny pieces of fruit cake.

'We thought you could explain our presence here to the – er – rest of the community,' said Eglington, warming his hands against a non-existent fire. 'So many foolish rumours can develop in a place like Five Oaks.'

'True. How true!' agreed the Reverend Grout, who often had more than his fair share of them. The Eglingtons had lived in India, where, Joshua told them, they'd become very friendly with a Colonel and Mrs. Thorne. The Thornes had both died of yellow fever within the same week, leaving an only daughter.

'Just before the Colonel passed away,' intoned Joshua lugubriously, 'he made us Cicely's guardians. We thought it best to bring her back to England. After all – this house belongs to her now.'

'India was no place for a girl of her tender years,' Edith added, pouring out some more weak tea for Squire Armstrong. 'Though we shall have to keep her somewhat . . . protected . . . from the outside world.'

'Protected?' repeated the Squire.

'The child is of – well – a very nervous disposition since the death of her parents,' Eglington explained. 'Sometimes she becomes . . . confused . . . even hysterical.' Joshua turned to Doctor Gordon. 'You would understand, of course.'

'Yes, of course,' said James, though he doubted the Eglingtons showed much sympathy towards the girl. They seemed to him a cold pair of fish.

'Perhaps, my dear, you could fetch Cicely now,' said Joshua to his sister. Edith glided out and he turned to the Vicar. 'We shall of course, attend church.' He looked at James. 'And consult you, Doctor, should it ever be necessary.'

'I hope it never is, Mr. Eglington,' James replied politely.

When Edith returned with Cicely, James looked closely at the girl. She was pale but controlled. James was unaware that her attempted escape had resulted in a savage beating. Eglington introduced her, and she curtsied to each of the guests in turn. 'The Reverend Grout, Mr. Armstrong, and Doctor Gordon,' rattled off Joshua. James gave her a friendly smile and she tried hard to smile back, but her lip trembled and her eyes filled with tears.

James felt sorry for the girl. She obviously missed her parents very much. Kevin's wild tale of prisoners and attempted escapes was all imagination.

So that night he went to their room – Albert was staying the weekend – and told them the facts. They were to keep away from Granley Hall.

'You still ain't convinced, are you?' said Albert after James had left.

'No,' Kevin replied, 'and I'm going back there tomorrow. Don't worry,' he added, as Albert gave a groan, 'I'm going by myself.'

The following afternoon Kevin took Black Beauty and galloped over to Granley Hall. He was excited by the possibility that he might see Cicely again. In his imagination, she had become a maiden in distress and he was one of the knights of old, Sir Galahad perhaps, riding his trusty steed to rescue her.

Cautiously he reached the wall round the house.

Then standing on Black Beauty's back, he peered over into the garden.

He could see Cicely sitting at a little table in the middle of the lawn, writing busily. Beside her were a pile of books. In the distance Kevin could see Edith Eglington watching from a window. As the woman turned away, he scrambled over the wall.

'Cicely!' Kevin called, careful that only she should hear him.

Cicely looked up sharply.

'Over here!' hissed Kevin.

Then Cicely saw him. She looked quickly at the house. Edith had left the window, so she stood up, opened a book, and, pretending to read from it, walked slowly over to Kevin's hiding place.

'They may be watching us,' she whispered.

'Your uncle and aunt?'

'How did you know?'

Kevin beckoned her to join him, and after another fearful glance at the house, Cicely came round to his hiding place. Kevin thought she looked even prettier than before. 'I'm Kevin Gordon,' he said. 'My father was here yesterday.'

'The nice doctor?' smiled Cicely.

'Well, he's nice sometimes—'

She took Kevin's arm. 'What did they tell him about me?'

Kevin looked uncomfortable. 'They said that you were ... that you were ...'

'Hysterical?' Cicely finished for him. 'Unbalanced?'

Kevin reddened and nodded his head. Cicely took his hand earnestly. 'What do you think?' she said.

'I don't believe it.'

Cicely was filled with hope. Here at last was someone who believed she was sane. She had suspected her guardians would lie to prevent her leaving Granley Hall without them, and thus make any escape impossible.

'Are they really your guardians?' Kevin asked.

'I don't know ... I don't think my parents even liked them. I certainly didn't. They were always trying to borrow money, but they never did anything to help when my parents became ill.'

'Have you any relatives?'

'Only my grandfather. I tried writing to him but Joshua tore up the letter, and now I have to write what he tells me, and it's all lies! I have to write how kind he is and how much I love Edith, and how happy I am . . .'

Cicely was crying so Kevin took a handkerchief from his pocket and gently dried her eyes. Then he put his arm round her and did his best to comfort her. 'Look,' he said, 'why not write to your grandfather now? I'll post it for you.'

Cicely brightened. Here was a chance to tell her grandfather how she really felt. Perhaps she could ask him to come to Granley Hall and see the way she was being treated.

'Cicely! Cicely! *Where are you?*'

It was Edith. Unable to see her ward, she had hurried from the house. Kevin and Cicely looked at each other in alarm then, without another word, the girl hurried back through the bushes while Kevin crouched low.

'Why did you leave your work?' asked Edith suspiciously.

Cicely showed her the book. 'Mr. Eglington told me to learn this sermon by heart and I find it easier if I walk about.'

Edith sniffed. 'I doubt if your governess will allow such perambulation,' she said icily.

Cicely was startled. 'My . . . . governess?'

'A distant cousin of mine will be arriving next week, and she is far less good natured than I.'

Hearing this, Kevin shuddered for he doubted anyone could be less kind than Edith.

'Continue your work!' she commanded Cicely, 'and remain seated.' She swept off to the house, her long skirts rustling over the grass.

Cicely began writing her letter while Kevin waited

patiently. He was alarmed when Edith sat on the terrace, making it impossible for Cicely to give him the letter. He reckoned without her ingenuity however. After addressing the letter she folded it into a paper dart, waited until Edith's attention was elsewhere, then launched the dart at Kevin's hiding place. It landed at his feet and when Edith looked down the garden, Cicely was reading again, while Kevin crept back to the wall.

He climbed over on to Black Beauty, who was restive. The horse whinnied. 'Be quiet, stupid!' whispered Kevin straightening out the letter and reading the address. Old Mr. Thorn lived in Norfolk, in the village of Bexwell. Beauty gave another warning neigh and Kevin looked up in surprise. Joshua Eglington was riding towards him. 'I'll take that!' he snapped. Mutely Kevin held out the letter and watched while Eglington tore it up.

'Your name, boy?' he demanded. He was very controlled but underneath he was seething with anger, and Kevin didn't like the way he clutched his whip. He made a sudden break for it. Beauty was quickly away and, luckily for Kevin, it took Eglington several seconds to recover before he spurred his horse into action. Kevin didn't want to be followed back to York Cottage, so he went by a devious route, and at length was able to lose him.

As he groomed Black Beauty in the stable, he told his story to Albert. His friend was fascinated: the whole thing was straight out of one of his penny dreadfuls. 'He must feel very sure of himself,' said Albert, 'tearing up the letter like that.'

'What letter?' said Doctor Gordon, coming into the stable without warning.

CHAPTER TWELVE

THE DECOY

Kevin had always been a very truthful boy and he knew his father would be easier on him if he made a clean breast of it. So he told him everything.

James realised that Kevin had disobeyed him because he was genuinely worried about the girl. The doctor had slight misgivings himself about the way she was being treated, so instead of being angry, he tried to reason with his son.

'First of all,' he said, 'you were trespassing. And secondly, the sudden shock of your appearance could have a disturbing effect on that poor girl.'

Doctor Gordon's restraint was met head on. 'There's nothing wrong with Cicely,' Kevin answered vehemently. 'She's frightened of the Eglington's that's all. And they told you all that "nervous and confused" stuff about her, just to keep her locked up. They even dictate the letters she writes!'

James, who felt that his attempt at friendship and understanding had been rejected, began to lose his temper. 'And why should they do all this?'

'I don't know!' Kevin almost shouted back. 'Neither does she. Why don't *we* write to her grandfather. I know the address. It's Bexwell in Norfolk—'

'It is nothing to do with us,' interrupted James angrily. 'And from now on – keep away from Granley Hall and have nothing more to do with Cicely. Nothing, do you understand?'

Kevin didn't reply; the only answer he gave was to turn on his heel and march out. It was an act of defiance but James was a wise father and didn't call him back. Besides the question of the letter had troubled him.

For a week, nobody mentioned Cicely at York Cottage and the atmosphere between father and son was somewhat strained. However, had James known what Kevin was planning, he would have been horrified. Albert felt his friend was up to something, and when he saw him slinking into the stable one day, he followed him.

Kevin was working away at what looked like a bundle of rope. He was so intent that he didn't notice Albert spying on him. Albert gave a little cough. Kevin looked up anxiously and relaxed when he saw who it was. Then he went on with his work.

'What's that?' asked Albert casually.

For answer Kevin spread out the rope. It was a ladder, and Albert began to be faintly worried. 'What's it for?'

'Cicely's escape,' said Kevin calmly, and tied another knot.

Albert rolled up his eyes in despair. 'You're not starting all that again, are you?'

'I never stopped,' Kevin answered. 'As a matter of fact, I've been watching the house for days, from a tree overlooking the grounds. Cicely studies in the garden for an hour every afternoon, and always between two o'clock and three. The ghouls keep an eye on her, but not all the time.'

Albert giggled. He liked the word ghouls. Then he looked serious again. 'You'll never bring it off.'

'Oh yes I will. I only need three more things to make it work.'

'What are they?'

'A bit of luck. Black Beauty. And *you*, Albert.'

Now Albert had no wish to take part – any part – in such a venture, and he said so firmly; but Kevin was determined he was going to help and over-rode all objections.

In the end Albert gave in. But when he was told exactly what part he had to play, he shook his head violently. 'I draw the line there Kevin – I really do!' he said indignantly. Nevertheless, by careful cajoling he was finally persuaded.

Two days later the pair of them went over to Granley Hall with Black Beauty and the rope ladder.

They reached the wall and waited until they heard the clock on Five Oaks church strike two. 'Now, any final questions?' whispered Kevin. Albert had one he wanted to ask. 'Well?' said Kevin.

'Can I go home?' said Albert.

Kevin was not amused. This was not the time for jokes, he thought, as he hooked the rope ladder to the wall and scrambled down into the garden. Albert followed him and together they hid in the bushes and waited anxiously for Cicely.

They hardly dared breathe and every tiny sound in the garden startled them. A ladybird crawled over Albert's hand. White butterflies danced in the dark green rhododendron leaves. They reminded Kevin of Cicely. She was a frightened butterfly, he thought, trapped in the Eglingtons' net. From the house came the distant rattle of tea cups. Somewhere a door banged. A starling flew on to the lawn, pecked spitefully at a sparrow and stole its food. To

Kevin the bird looked very like Joshua.

'I don't think she's coming,' whispered Albert, almost hopefully. But Kevin had seen her and he gripped Albert's arm. Edith was with her ward and waited until she began her work before returning to the house.

As if preparing for his execution Albert removed his jacket . . .

Indoors, Joshua Eglington was going through the house-keeping accounts. As he checked the lists he would pause every now and then and pencil a precise question mark against some item he regarded as either unnecessary or extravagant. From his window he could look out to the distant figure on the lawn. It gave him intense satisfaction to sit at Colonel Thorne's desk, surrounded by his property, and know that in a few years it would be all his.

Edith rustled silkily into the room. 'Henrietta should be arriving shortly,' she purred.

'Splendid,' replied Joshua. 'She'll soon break the girl's spirit.'

Cicely was walking backwards and forwards across the lawn, apparently deep in a book. 'A few years of Henrietta's discipline,' Joshua went on, 'and the little fool will do anything we say when she comes of age.'

The Eglingtons smiled at one another and turned away from the window. So they did not see Cicely pass out of sight behind the rhododendrons. 'As long as she *signs* everything . . .' murmured Edith.

'Oh, I'm sure she will,' replied her brother. 'We certainly won't need to commit *another* forgery.' They chuckled together over their secret. As Cicely's parents lay dying, the Eglingtons had stolen Colonel Thorne's will and forged a new one and appointed themselves the girl's guardians. By the time she was 21 they planned to make her so frightened and subservient, she would do anything they asked, even to signing away her inheritance. The wicked pair were so busy laughing at their own cleverness and deceit, they failed to notice Cicely was no longer in view.

They would have been very surprised if they had seen their ward – now in her bodice and petticoats – putting on Albert's jacket and being hurried by Kevin to the rope ladder.

Cicely was very bewildered by the suddenness and ease of her escape; she climbed the ladder, Kevin helped her down on to Black Beauty and they started for home. 'We've done it!' he cried, as they galloped down the lane. 'They'll never catch us now!'

Near York Cottage, Kevin dismounted and helped his 'rescued maiden' to the ground. 'What about Albert?' she asked anxiously.

'Beauty'll fetch him,' Kevin replied with a smile.

Cicely thought he was joking for a moment but her laughter stopped when Black Beauty turned back at Kevin's command.

Meanwhile Henrietta Eglington had arrived at Granley Hall. Even Joshua and Edith were daunted by her severe appearance. She was tall and gaunt, and a ruthless air surrounded her. Her long boney face was crowned by an ornate black hat so full of bits and pieces of net and lace and feathers it might have been a vulture's nest.

'Ah, my dear,' said Joshua ingratiatingly, 'I hope you had a pleasant journey.'

'No,' replied his cousin disagreeably – she had come by train and been forced to travel third class – 'it was a most uncomfortable experience. Where is the girl?'

Joshua pointed to the distant figure in the garden. 'I will fetch her,' he replied.

But Henrietta said she would prefer to meet Cicely alone. 'First impressions are most important,' she snapped. 'Kindly show me to the garden, Edith.'

Albert, sitting with his breeches rolled up above his knees, and wearing Cicely's dress and bonnet, was beginning to feel very uneasy. He was not only a decoy duck but a sitting one as well, and he seemed to have been sitting for a long time. Surely Kevin was clear by now? He crossed his legs under the skirt, remembered he was supposed to be a girl, and uncrossed them again. Then to his horror he saw Henrietta bearing down like a storm cloud.

'Good afternoon, Cicely,' she said grimly, 'I am your new governess.' To Albert her voice seemed loaded with doom. Had she announced that the end of the world was to be that afternoon, he could not have been more panic-stricken. He thought wildly of escape, but he doubted his legs would support him, if he tried to get up. But Henrietta was determined that he should. She was outraged by Cicely's bad manners. 'Stand up, girl!' she ordered.

The venom in her voice shot Albert to his feet like a rocket. He stood stiffly to attention, Cicely's bonnet at a rakish angle.

Even using her lorgnettes, Henrietta was rather short sighted; she looked distastefully through them at her new pupil. 'So *you* are Cicely?' she said.

Albert nodded miserably.

'Curtsey!'

Albert bobbed up and down quickly.

'I am appalled by your untidy appearance and your

positively dreadful manners. I can see I've arrived not a moment too soon. How old are you?'

The awful moment had arrived, for now Albert had to speak. He folded his hands, licked his lips and mumbled faintly that he was fifteen.

Henrietta glared at him. As well as being shortsighted she was also a bit deaf. 'Speak up!' she snapped.

'Fifteen!' bellowed Albert, going very red in the face.

'Have you a cold?' inquired Henrietta icily, slightly taken aback by the girl's deep voice.

Albert clutched at the proffered straw. 'Er . . . yes . . . miss . . . and it's somethink chronic.'

'Then it is obvious you spend far too much time out of doors.' The lorgnettes went under Albert's chin and his head was tilted back. 'Your complexion is very unsatisfactory,' Henrietta concluded.

Out of the corner of his eye, Albert saw Joshua and Edith coming across the lawn and tried to back away.

'Stand still!' snapped the martinet.

'What, and get nabbed by them two?' gasped Albert, his nerve completely shattered.

Henrietta was appalled. Never before had a girl spoken to her so rudely, but Albert was past caring what she thought. He made to run, trod on his skirt and crashed to the ground. The dress rucked up revealing his boots and breeches. Henrietta gave a scream worthy of a prima donna and began whacking him with her parasol.

Albert scrambled up and charged into the bushes, his skirts held high. 'It's a boy! It's a boy!' shrieked Henrietta and promptly went into hysterics.

With Eglington close behind him, Albert raced for the rope ladder but was hampered by his skirt. Eglington

Your complexion is very unsatisfactory

grabbed him but after a brief scuffle Albert broke from him and charged back past Edith and Henrietta. As he burst through the rhododendron bush, Henrietta began screaming again and Edith joined in. Thoroughly unnerved, Albert veered off towards the house. But Evans, the coachman, was there. He had heard the hubbub and come to investigate. Albert ducked down another path with both men just behind him. Like a circus clown going through a hoop, he dived at a privet hedge, crashed out the other side, tumbled head over heels, ran back to the rope ladder, pulled off the dress, and climbed to the top of the wall.

It was a long way to drop but Evans was already running to the rope ladder. Albert launched himself from the wall. He landed heavily, hurting his ankle, and limped off as fast as he was able.

Some way from the house he looked back: his head sank, for Eglington and Evans were following him on horseback and he had no chance of getting away.

Then, as if by magic, Black Beauty was cantering up to him. Albert had never known a more welcome sight, and he prayed the horse would reach him first.

Eglington and his servant were coming up fast, but so was Beauty, and Beauty was going like the wind. He reached Albert when Eglington and his man were barely yards away, and the boy – a cunning rider – leapt on his back.

If Albert had pulled up Beauty to turn him, he would have been caught. He knew this, so instead he rode straight at his pursuers. The unexpected trick worked. He shot between the riders, who pulled up in confusion; and by the time they'd recovered, Albert was well clear.

'Let him go, Evans!' cried Joshua Eglington with evil triumph. 'We've no need to follow him. The horse, Evans, the horse! Did you mark it? 'T'was the same that the other young ruffian rode. And I knew then that I'd seen it before. In our stable, Evans! The stable of Granley Hall! *When Doctor James Gordon came to tea!*'

So Albert's ruse to lead them on a false trail failed because Black Beauty had been recognised; and Joshua Eglington rode to York Cottage.

Kevin had hidden Cicely in the stable. He was talking innocently to his father when Eglington and Evans clattered into the yard. 'Where's your fine black horse, Doctor Gordon?' Eglington demanded. 'And where's my ward?'

'Well, Kevin? Where is Cicely?' James asked imperturbably. His manner puzzled Kevin for James seemed very calm about the whole affair. Sadly, he fetched Cicely from her hiding place. She was very pale, but determined not to cry, and she faced Eglington bravely.

'I've a good mind to see you struck off, Gordon. And your children sent to prison!' said Joshua viciously.

'Why not, Mr. Eglington?' said James. 'Take the matter to court and prosecute the lot of us!'

Kevin and Cicely looked at him in amazement and so did Joshua Eglington. He recovered quickly though, and ignoring Doctor Gordon, ordered Cicely to join him.

'Stay where you are Cicely!' said James.

'Get her, Evans!' Joshua snarled.

Evans dismounted but James stepped in front of the girl protectively. 'You are not to lay a hand on her,' he said quietly but so firmly that Evans was cowed.

Then James took a letter from his pocket. 'Perhaps this might interest you,' he said to Eglington. 'It's from a

Colonel Thorne of Bexwell in Norfolk.'

Kevin could hardly believe it – his father had written after all!

'Yes, Kevin, I wrote to him,' James went on. 'Your . . . "investigations" . . . had made me suspicious. I told Mr. Thorne of Cicely's unhappiness, and how you, sir,' – and here he looked hard at Eglington again – 'prevented her writing to him.'

'Lies!' Eglington almost screamed the word. 'Lies made up by this hysterical and weak-minded girl!'

James waited calmly for the outburst to cease before he continued. 'Mr. Thorne intends coming to see you. He wishes to have his son's will examined by experts, as he suspects it to be a forgery.'

This silenced Eglington completely and everyone could see he was very shaken. He licked his lips, suddenly dry with fear, and his claw-like hands began to tremble.

'Until then,' James said. 'Cicely will remain here with us.' He put away the letter and spoke clearly and decisively to Joshua Eglington for the last time. 'Leave my property at once or *I'll* prosecute *you*—' and here he winked at Kevin – 'for trespass.'

Eglington knew his crime would be discovered and that a prison sentence awaited him. His shoulders sagged and in silence he turned away.

As the two men left the yard, Albert galloped up on Black Beauty but Eglington hardly noticed him.

Kevin was hugging Cicely and Doctor Gordon was smiling broadly. 'Well, somebody tell me what happened!' said Albert.

That night, in the warm darkness of the stable, Black

Beauty heard the sound of laughter coming from the cottage; and later, the piano being played and the children's voices singing.

He knew them all so well: Jenny's sweet treble, Kevin's husky tones, and the confident out-of-tune noise made by Ned and Albert.

He looked at Jonah but the little pony was already asleep. An owl hooted and swooped low searching the yard for mice. The hayfields were bright with moonlight and in the distance Five Oaks church clock began to chime. At Eddington Hall, Squire Armstrong poured out another glass of port. In The Two Foxes, P.C. Dickens downed his pint of ale.

The children sang on, and presently Amy's contralto and Doctor Gordon's strong bass joined in. Black Beauty's eyes closed, and he slept.